"You up for an early dinner?"

She sent him a pointed look, her grip on the dash loosening. "If it means you'll stop driving like a crazy person."

He laughed. The sedan by now would be waiting for them at their hotel since he wasn't able to keep up. "Sorry about that, but we had a tail, and I wanted to give him a hard time."

She groaned. "They're already watching us?"

"They are. Actually, I'm surprised it took this long." He flashed her a smile. "But this is good."

Anne made a face. "If you say so."

"It means they're worried," he explained. "If they had nothing to hide, they wouldn't be worried."

She turned to him, and a smile spread across her pretty face. "You're right. This is good."

Reader Note

Jamie Colby is learning from the best, her grandmother Victoria. I hope you'll enjoy this young woman's journey to blazing her own path. I can't wait to see where Jamie takes the Colby Agency. Enjoy!

MEMORY OF MURDER

DEBRA WEBB

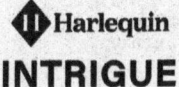
INTRIGUE

If you purchased this book without a cover you should be aware that this book is stolen property. It was reported as "unsold and destroyed" to the publisher, and neither the author nor the publisher has received any payment for this "stripped book."

ISBN-13: 978-1-335-08208-4

Memory of Murder

Copyright © 2025 by Debra Webb

All rights reserved. No part of this book may be used or reproduced in any manner whatsoever without written permission.

Without limiting the author's and publisher's exclusive rights, any unauthorized use of this publication to train generative artificial intelligence (AI) technologies is expressly prohibited.

This is a work of fiction. Names, characters, places and incidents are either the product of the author's imagination or are used fictitiously. Any resemblance to actual persons, living or dead, businesses, companies, events or locales is entirely coincidental.

For questions and comments about the quality of this book, please contact us at CustomerService@Harlequin.com.

TM and ® are trademarks of Harlequin Enterprises ULC.

Harlequin Enterprises ULC
22 Adelaide St. West, 41st Floor
Toronto, Ontario M5H 4E3, Canada
www.Harlequin.com

Printed in U.S.A.

Debra Webb is the award-winning, *USA TODAY* bestselling author of more than one hundred novels, including those in reader-favorite series Faces of Evil, the Colby Agency and Shades of Death. With more than four million books sold in numerous languages and countries, Debra has a love of storytelling that goes back to her childhood on a farm in Alabama. Visit Debra at debrawebb.com.

Books by Debra Webb

Harlequin Intrigue

Colby Agency: The Next Generation

A Colby Christmas Rescue
Alibi for Murder
Memory of Murder

Lookout Mountain Mysteries

Disappearance in Dread Hollow
Murder at Sunset Rock
A Place to Hide
Whispering Winds Widows
Peril in Piney Woods

A Winchester, Tennessee Thriller

In Self Defense
The Dark Woods
The Stranger Next Door
The Safest Lies
Witness Protection Widow
Before He Vanished
The Bone Room

Visit the Author Profile page at Harlequin.com.

CAST OF CHARACTERS

Anne Griffin — She was born in prison and grew up bouncing from one foster care home to the next. She has no family...only the label of being a murderer's daughter. But she's made something of her life all on her own. Does she really want to know the whole truth about her past?

Jack Brenner — He's one of the Colby Agency's best at solving cold cases. But can he hold on to his heart while he navigates this decades-old mystery?

Mary Morton — She spent more than half her life in prison for a murder she didn't commit. Can she trust the Colby Agency to find the truth...even after she's dead?

Neil Reed — The murder victim. The father of Mary Morton's baby...the man she loved.

Eve and Kevin Langston — Best friends of Mary and Neil...or were they?

Carin Carter Wallace — Friend or gold digger?

Preston Reed — Neil was his son. He hated Mary because she took everything from him.

Victoria Colby-Camp — The head of the Colby Agency. Victoria never backs down from danger.

Jamie Colby — Victoria's granddaughter and the future of the Colby Agency.

Chapter One

Chicago
Monday, July 7
Colby Agency, 9:30 a.m.

Jamie Colby waited in her grandmother's office, the package sitting in her lap. Her fingers tapped out a tune on the box that had gotten slightly battered in transit. The package and its contents had been in Jamie's possession for a mere three days, but already she was convinced of what needed to be done. Quickly, she reminded herself. This had to happen as soon as possible.

Somehow she would make the indomitable Victoria Colby-Camp see that her plan was a good one. A necessary one that had to be carried out, even if pro bono. The agency did pro bono work all the time. Did it really matter that the actual client was deceased?

Not in Jamie's opinion. The woman deserved to have her reputation restored. Some things transcended death.

The door opened, and Victoria breezed into the office and settled behind her desk. "Good morning." She smiled brightly as she always did whenever she saw Jamie for the first time each day.

Jamie adored her grandmother. Her entire life Jamie had always known she wanted to be just like her.

No matter that she and Jamie had been working together now for nearly seven months, each day was like the first with her grandmother. Calling Victoria *Grandmother* almost always put off anyone who met them for the first time. Primarily because Victoria looked far younger than her seventy-two years. The silver threaded through her black hair spoke of sophistication and wisdom rather than age. But it was her keen eyes that warned she was no little old lady.

Jamie smiled. "Good morning, Grandmother."

Victoria eyed the package in Jamie's lap. "I understand you have a special case under consideration."

So, Ian had spoken to her already. Jamie wasn't surprised. It wasn't as if she had told him not to tell Victoria. Perhaps he'd hoped to grease the wheels, so to speak. Ian Michaels was one of her grandmother's closest friends and colleagues. His recommendation would go a long way—assuming he leaned in Jamie's favor, and she suspected he would.

"Yes." Jamie stood. She placed the box on the edge of her grandmother's desk and removed the contents piece by piece. First the handwritten journal. Then the photos, the newspaper clippings, a locket, Polaroid-type photos and the baby blanket—the sort of receiving blanket given at birth, usually by a hospital. A detailed letter from the accused killer had accompanied the box.

As Victoria shuffled through the photos, Jamie explained, "Mary Morton was charged with first-degree murder thirty years ago. She was sentenced to life in prison. At the time she was pregnant, and the baby—a girl—was later born and subsequently taken from her. Since Mary had no other family or close friends able or willing to take the child, she was introduced into the foster system."

Victoria moved on to the newspaper clippings. "Has the child—woman," she amended, "been contacted about her mother's death?"

Jamie nodded. "I spoke with the warden. He gives his best, by the way." Her grandmother knew everyone who was anyone in key positions in the state and no small number of VIPs across the country. "A notification was sent to her last known address. I checked out the address, and she does live there. There's every reason to believe she's aware of the situation."

Victoria reached for the journal. "Tell me why we should be interested in this convicted murderer's history."

Jamie resumed her seat. "At the time of the murder, Mary Morton was twenty-four years old. She had just completed her master's in teaching, and she was already employed at an elementary school in Crystal Lake. On a personal level, she was engaged to a law student set to graduate the upcoming year. His name was Neil Reed. Both Mary and Neil grew up in Crystal Lake. Her parents were deceased, but his still lived in the area."

"Reed was the victim in the murder case." Victoria placed the journal with the other items.

Obviously her grandmother had already looked into the details. Possibly a good sign.

"Yes. Mary insisted throughout the trial that she was innocent, but the preponderance of evidence was overwhelming. Her prints were on the murder weapon. She had blood on her clothes. Her court-appointed attorney—a man swamped with cases—didn't stand a chance against the newly elected hotshot district attorney determined to make a name for himself. My impression is that the case was decided even before a jury was selected."

Victoria picked up a newspaper clipping, considered it a moment. "Why are we talking about this case, Jamie? The poor woman, guilty or innocent, is dead. I really don't see how we can help her."

"We can," Jamie countered. "Mary's greatest regret was that she couldn't clear her name to prove to her only child that she was not the daughter of a murderer. According to her letter, Mary didn't care if she was ever released. She only wanted to clear her name for her daughter's sake. Her attorney promised to appeal her conviction, but his meager efforts proved futile. Still Mary never gave up. No matter how earnest her efforts, it was as if whatever legal maneuvers she attempted were doomed from the outset. Every single time she was met with defeat. No reporter ever showed interest in her story. Fate simply turned a blind eye to her. I feel strongly that the justice system let her down."

Victoria studied Jamie. "Or she was simply guilty and no one wanted to help change a righteous verdict."

"That's possible, yes. However, everyone—even the guilty—has the right to petition for an appeal. But guilt is not the sense I'm getting from what we have here." Jamie gestured to the contents of the box spread over her grandmother's desk. "Just before she died, Mary had lost all hope. She saw an article about you, Grandmother, and the story gave her hope that there were still good people in the world who might be able to help her. She put together this package and asked that it be mailed to our office. An indifferent guard never bothered to see that it was done. But after her death, there was some question about why all her personal items were missing, and another guard discovered the box in an office. She checked the contents and then hand delivered it here."

Victoria continued to study her, waiting, apparently, for her to go on.

"After a thorough examination of all you see, and a review of the available public information on the case, I feel compelled to open a case and assign an investigator."

"Who do you have in mind?" Victoria leaned forward and placed the items back in the box.

"Jack Brenner. He has extensive experience with cold cases. I believe if there is something to be found, he can find it."

Victoria sat back once more and resumed her analysis of Jamie. "Jack is an excellent choice."

Anticipation flared. "Is that a yes?"

"On one condition," Victoria pointed out.

Hesitation slowed Jamie's mental victory celebration. "What condition?"

"The daughter will be notified and asked to participate in the investigation. We're not going to do this without giving her an opportunity for input. In fact, I would prefer she be actively involved."

Jamie nodded. "Fair enough."

"Brief Jackson," Victoria went on. "When he's ready have him reach out to the daughter and make an appointment to discuss the possibility."

Jamie stood. "Very well." She placed the items back into the box and picked it up. "Thank you. You won't regret your decision."

"I'm sure I won't."

VICTORIA SMILED AS the door closed behind Jamie. For a while Victoria had worried about her. Jamie was so young. The commitment here at the agency was different from her previous work with the government. It was far more personal. Often, the inexperienced in the field of private investigations poured their hearts and souls into the work on a level that was impossible to maintain for any length of time. Victoria knew that her granddaughter would do this. The best investigators always gave their all but paced themselves for the long haul. That skill came with time. Surprisingly, Jamie had found a good balance very quickly.

Having Jamie here had fulfilled Victoria's longtime dream that her grandchildren would one day take over. Both Jamie and her brother Luke had seemed intent on different career paths. To have Jamie make this leap had been an incredible joy. Particularly since Jim, Victoria's son and Jamie and Luke's father, was still helping their mother, Tasha, recover from her horrendous illness, and quite frankly, he had no desire to take the position as head of the agency. He had made himself clear on that point some time ago and had not changed his mind. The need for Jamie to come onboard had never been more apparent, but Victoria had not wanted to push the idea on the girl—young woman.

Jamie was here now and seemed immensely happy with her work. The fact that she had taken the initiative on a somewhat delicate situation warmed Victoria's heart. Jamie was going to make an amazing leader for this agency one day.

Victoria could not wait to share this news with Lucas. Her husband had insisted all along that Jamie was happy at the agency, but Victoria had allowed a few doubts to seep in. Lucas remained convinced that having Kenny—Kendrick Poe—on board at the agency with Jamie had helped to ensure her continued happiness. Kenny, too, was a great asset. Victoria often wondered how long it would be before Jamie and Kenny took their relationship to the next level. Victoria's heart thumped faster at the idea of a Colby wedding.

There were times when her seventh decade of life seemed to fly by so very fast that she couldn't help but wonder about all she would miss when she was gone. But then she reminded herself that it was far more important to stay focused on not missing anything today than to worry about what she might miss tomorrow.

She pushed back her chair and walked to the window overlooking the street below. The Chicago weather was particularly warm, even in July.

She smiled. The future looked exactly as she had hoped it would.

Chapter Two

Aurora, Illinois
Tuesday, July 8
Griffin Residence
Borkshire Lane, 1:30 p.m.

Anne Griffin smiled as she ended the call. The job was hers!

Her smile stretched into a happy, relieved, grateful grin. "I got the job!"

She tossed her cell phone onto her desk, set her hands on her hips and walked to the window that overlooked her small, enclosed backyard. A celebratory cocktail and a few minutes of relaxing was in order, she decided. The weather was perfect, and that new chaise lounge on her little flagstone patio was calling her name.

With a deep breath, she padded to the kitchen and prepared her favorite drink. Three fresh strawberries went into the glass, along with a generous serving of lemonade and then a splash of vodka. Just a little. It was early for a cocktail, but it was nice to celebrate now and then. After all, this was her first really big contract since going out on her own at the beginning of the year.

These last few months had been a bit of an uphill climb, professionally speaking. Thankfully she'd been prepared for a period of little or no income. But recently, knowing her savings would soon be gone had her a little nervous. Luckily, she had also braced herself for the doubts that would arise.

How many times had she second-guessed her decision? Far too many. It was the curse of a worrier.

She lifted her glass in a silent toast. But all those uncertainties were behind her now. Griffin Interior Concepts was officially off the ground and running. Her scant client list was expanding. So far most of the work had been smaller scale—a kitchen or bath remodel, the occasional principal bedroom and one over-the-top screened-in porch. But this contract was big. Really big, as in a whole-house renovation. The owners had narrowed their choices to three designers, and Anne had been one of them. Two weeks ago, all three designers had submitted fully developed plans and cost estimates. To be honest, she'd been incredibly thankful to even be in the running.

And now the job was hers.

She did a happy dance and then sipped her drink. A little sun was in order. Far too much time was spent behind her desk lately so she wandered out to her patio. Her home was an end-unit town house, with a patio slightly larger than most. She had a square of flagstone for entertaining and a little patch of grass. Shrubbery and flowers formed a pleasing border against the fence. It was really quite lovely. She couldn't complain. Frankly, any more than this would take up too much of her time in maintenance. Building a business, she needed every available minute to keep the momentum going. One day, when she had more employees to do the leg work, she wouldn't mind having a larger home and garden.

"One day," she repeated aloud.

With a sigh, she settled onto the chaise lounge and enjoyed her fruity drink. After she figured out a late lunch she would take a drive to the exclusive neighborhood where her first whole-house reno would be taking place. A few more shots of the home wouldn't hurt. Maybe a walk around the block.

Another grin tugged at her lips. Taking on the project would be like buying a major ad campaign. This couple was very involved in the community. The wife was a social media influencer, so she would certainly use the renovation as fodder for her numerous posts and reels. The couple socialized in real life a lot as well. Their big parties were widely known—and promoted on her media pages. Anne couldn't be more delighted at the idea of how much publicity this one job would provide. To top it off, she was being paid particularly well for the work. A truly win-win situation.

For the next few moments, she considered the steps she needed to take moving forward. She would make a call to each of her go-to contractors and see how this job would fit into their schedules. There was at least one floor tile she would need to get ordered as soon as possible. Thankfully the scheduling of contractors wouldn't be much of a problem. The clients were busy people who traveled a good deal of the time, particularly in the summer. So getting the work done wouldn't be nearly as difficult as it was when clients were home, trying to live and/or work around construction. That part was always tricky.

The doorbell drew Anne's attention back to the present. It was a miracle she'd heard it. As she got to her feet she noted that she'd left the French doors ajar, which was likely the only reason she had. Knowing her new client, it could very well be a congratulatory flower delivery.

She walked inside, finished off her drink and

put the glass in the sink before making her way to the front door. One of the things she loved about this town home was that the entire downstairs was one large open space. There was a short hallway that led to a powder room and drop zone for coats and shoes, but all else was wide open. The floating staircase to the left of the front door led up to an exposed second-floor hallway and the bedrooms—one of which she had turned into an office.

It was everything she needed while staying in budget.

Budgets were particularly important when deciding to go into business for oneself.

Before opening the door, she checked through the security viewfinder to get a look at the visitor.

Male. Tall. Dark hair. Broad shoulders. Navy trousers with a matching lightweight business jacket, pale blue button-down shirt, open at the throat. No flowers anywhere to be seen.

Salesman, maybe.

Then she spotted the box in his right hand. Perhaps a deliveryman? If so, he was a bit overdressed for the occasion. It wasn't her birthday, so it wouldn't be a surprise gift from one of her colleagues.

"May I help you?" she asked through the door.

"Afternoon, Ms. Griffin." He smiled.

Deep voice. Pleasant smile. Handsome. A little flutter in her belly reminded her that while pinching pennies for this independent business launch, she'd also neglected all forms of social life.

"I'm Jackson Brenner. I work with the Colby Agency." He removed his wallet from a hip pocket and held his credentials up to the viewfinder. She stared at the photo that was indeed him. "I'd like to speak with you, if you have a few minutes."

The Colby Agency. A frown furrowed her brow. She had no idea what sort of business he represented. "I'm afraid you have me at a disadvantage, Mr. Brenner. I don't know what your agency is or does."

Certainly, she had no clue why someone from said agency would be at her door. Unless he was selling insurance or something else she did not need.

"The Colby Agency is a private investigations firm, ma'am. I'm here about your mother, Mary Morton."

Anne drew back as if the words had been stones flung at her. A barrage of confusing emotions twisted inside her. Mary Morton was dead. Why would anyone be contacting Anne now? Surely there was some mistake.

"I was informed that she passed away." Anne eased closer to the viewfinder once more.

"Yes, ma'am. That's why I'm here. Your mother left some personal items intended for you."

Anne's gaze shifted to the box once more. She bit her lip. From time to time since she was a teenager she had been approached by reporters, even a private detective once. All had wanted to question her about her mother and the murder. None had wanted to help Mary Morton in any way. It was all for documentaries or books that served only the person pursuing the research. The best stories were always about coldhearted monsters, and the hope had been that Anne would reiterate that idea about her biological mother.

In reality, Anne knew nothing about the murder or her biological mother. She had never met Mary Morton. Obviously when she was born in that prison infirmary she had been with her mother for a brief time. Not for even a moment since then. They had never met and they had never spoken. Anne had nothing to add to the woman's painfully sad story.

"I'm afraid I'm not clear on what it is you're delivering." She still wasn't ready to open the door and deal with whatever this unexpected visit actually involved.

"I understand your hesitancy, ma'am." His voice was soft, his face kind. "But I assure you this is something you will want to see and hear." He shrugged. "Otherwise I wouldn't be knocking on your door. The agency doesn't do this sort of thing unless there is a very good reason."

Anne drew back once more. What could it hurt? She would hear what he had to say, accept the box and then send him on his way. Ten minutes at most. She still had to call her assistant, Lisa, and tell her the good news about the contract. There was much she had to do. A stroll into a past she didn't recall or understand was not part of her agenda for the day.

Determined not to allow this strange development to dampen her spirits, Anne opened the door. *Just get it over with and move on.* Once he was on his way, she could go back to celebrating.

"Come in." She opened the door wider.

He entered, glanced around, then set his gaze on hers. "Thank you."

Anne closed the door and walked to the center of the room where the sofa and two chairs surrounded a coffee table and fronted a fireplace.

"Have a seat." She settled into her favorite chair and mentally braced for whatever he had to say.

He placed the box on the coffee table and lowered onto the sofa.

"What's in the box?" No need to wait for

him to begin. The sooner the conversation was started the sooner it would be done.

"Your mother's personal items."

Her gaze shifted from him to the box. It was a relatively small box. Apparently her biological mother's life had been reduced to this. She swallowed, annoyed at the tightness in her throat. "I received a letter from Logan Correctional Center informing me of her death. Why didn't they send this box at that time?" Wasn't that the typical way it was done? Personal effects were mailed to the next of kin.

"Your mother—"

"Wait." She held up a hand. "It's true that Mary Morton was my biological mother." Anne took a moment, drew in a steadying breath. "But that's all she was to me. We never met. Never spoke. She never wrote to me. Twenty-nine years ago, all she left me was alone. I went from the prison infirmary to a hospital and then to a foster family. From there I bounced from one family to the next. No one wanted to adopt the child of a murderer. So, honestly, I genuinely have no desire to receive anything from her now."

Now that she thought about it, why had she even opened the door? All those emotions from her earliest childhood memories flooded her: Disappointment. Sadness. Fear. Hatred. More fear.

He nodded. "I understand how you might

feel that way. But my dilemma is that the Colby Agency received a request from Ms. Morton, and we have an obligation to honor it."

Somehow Anne couldn't see her mother's name in the same sentence with the word *honor*, but there it was.

"In that case," she relented, "just get it over with. What's in the box, and why did you feel compelled to hand deliver it?"

The man—Jackson Brenner—reached out and opened the flaps of the box. "Inside you'll find a detailed journal, newspaper clippings and a few items I imagine were precious to your—to Ms. Morton."

Anne stood, crossed the four feet to the table and picked up the box. She took it back to her chair and sat it in her lap. Inside, the item on top was the journal. She picked it up and flipped through the pages. She wanted to remain unaffected, but the handwriting—her mother's handwriting—shifted something deep inside her even when she wanted desperately not to feel anything at all.

She was not your mother. The words echoed through her soul. Somehow holding that journal... She couldn't chase away the idea so easily.

"Five months before you were born," Jackson explained, "your mother was charged with the murder of Neil Reed. All who knew the two, who were engaged at the time, considered them the perfect couple. There hadn't been any trouble between Neil and Mary, and both had good reputations at their places of employment and in the community."

"Until the murder," Anne spoke up, setting the journal aside. Her skin seemed to tingle from touching it. A glutton for punishment, she reached for the next item in the box—newspaper clippings.

"Yes," Jackson agreed. "In her letter to my employer, Ms. Morton urged us to find the truth. She insisted that no one had even tried in all these years. At the time she wrote the letter she was aware that her time was limited. She'd just learned she had cancer. Her request was a final attempt to prod someone into finding the truth. Though it wouldn't help her, she hoped it would be of some comfort to you to learn that your mother was not a murderer."

The impact of his words hit her hard. Anne rode out the unsettling emotions, then grabbed back her protective shield. "Well, I'm afraid she will be very disappointed. You see, when I was nineteen I suddenly felt I needed to know the whole story. So I did a little digging myself. I have to say that I found nothing to indicate she was innocent. In fact, everything I discovered suggested the opposite. I can't imagine that you will find anything different."

"Perhaps I won't." He shrugged. "But I will look. I won't stop until I have irrefutable evidence one way or the other. She deserves that confirmation."

Deserves. Anne considered the idea for a moment. How was it that this stranger could believe a woman he didn't know deserved anything?

"What does this have to do with me?" Anne didn't want to sound uncaring, but frankly, she was. She had no reason to feel anything for this woman. In fact, she remembered well the moment when she had stopped feeling anything. It had been her twelfth birthday. All those years—at every birthday—she had told herself that would be the day her mother would come for her. She would be released from prison, and she would finally come to reclaim the child taken from her.

Except that never happened.

She never even sent a letter offering happy birthday to her only child.

And on her twelfth birthday, after running away from her newest foster home, Anne had understood that her mother was never coming. The fairy tale she had told herself as a child was nothing more than a self-comforting technique designed to keep the overwhelming sadness at bay.

No one was coming—least of all her mother.

"I won't pursue your mother's last request if you ask me not to." Jackson startled her from the painful thoughts. "If you tell me to let it go, I will. Those are my instructions from the top. This investigation won't move forward without your approval. I do, however, believe that if that is your decision, you will one day come to regret it."

Oh, she saw the endgame now. "Am I supposed to pay for this endeavor?" She almost laughed. Please. Absolutely no way. Was this Colby Agency nothing more than some shameful version of ambulance chasers?

"No," he assured her. "There is no fee involved with this investigation. But I do need your approval to move forward. Victoria made that point very clear."

"Victoria?" His boss, she presumed.

"The head of the Colby Agency."

Anne's first inclination was to say no. She did not agree with this ridiculous idea. She did not want the stuff in the box. She surely did not feel an obligation to the woman who gave birth to her.

But then she saw the photo. An old Polaroid-style photograph of a woman holding a tiny baby.

Her, she realized.

This was probably the only photo of her and her mother together that existed. Something pink grabbed her attention then. She touched it. A baby blanket.

The rip in her chest was abrupt, painful. Anne willed the sharp sensation away. The ache...the lost hope and childish desperation refused to go.

"Really," she insisted even as her throat tightened further. "I don't care. Do what she asked. It makes no difference to me." She tossed the photo back into the box and struggled to tamp down the emotions shearing through her. This woman—this murderer—would not cause her more pain. Not now. Not ever again.

He nodded. "There's just one catch, you see. In order to proceed we need your cooperation."

Her gaze narrowed on the man who had intruded on her day. "What does that mean? My cooperation?"

"Victoria feels strongly that I shouldn't move forward with my investigation unless you agree to be a part of the investigation."

No way. Anne would not go digging around in a past she knew nothing about for a woman who was a stranger to her.

Absolutely no way.

Chapter Three

3:00 p.m.

Anne watched from the front window as Jackson Brenner drove away.

Despite her misgivings, she had assured him that she would have an answer in the morning.

On some level she wanted to simply say no. Mary Morton didn't deserve the time of day from Anne, much less a day or more of her life. The very idea was ludicrous. But in her current emotional state, Anne didn't trust herself to make the right decision. As he so cleverly pointed out, she didn't want to have future regrets.

As soon as the man from the Colby Agency had walked out the door she had called the one person she trusted—her friend and personal assistant, Lisa Gilbert. Lisa was on her way over.

Anne crossed to the chair she had vacated and picked up the box.

The box.

It sounded so ominous...as if her mother's ashes or some dark secret were ensconced inside.

Her mother. Anne moved her head side to side. She had no mother. This woman—the biological mother—had never been a mother to her. None of the foster moms had been anything more than a supervisor. Anne felt confident there were good foster parents out there. Probably plenty of them. Sadly she had never been placed with a good one. She closed her eyes and pushed away the memories that tried to surface. Maybe her long run of bad luck had been in part due to the attitude she developed by age three, but mostly, she was certain, it was about her being the child of a murderer—born in prison.

No one had wanted her.

Anne forced her eyes open and kicked aside all those painful feelings. She had survived. And eventually she had thrived. All on her own, damn it.

Lips tight with frustration, she picked up the box and carried it to the dining area. Unlike many who kept some sort of decor on the table, Anne left hers clean for the purpose of spreading out her work. The one she'd chosen was larger than her sofa, its size necessary since she used it as a multipurpose piece. Although her office was upstairs, she often worked here with the French doors open so she could enjoy the fresh air. Not this time of year, obviously, because it was too hot. Open doors or not, she regularly used this as a conference table for meetings with clients. With Lisa on her way to *confer*, Anne removed the items from the box and spread them out over the tabletop as if they were samples related to a potential customer.

Flooring, paint, cabinetry... All sorts of sample pieces ended up on her table during a brainstorming session with Lisa or a meeting with clients. Generally, there were photographs of the space in need of a redo. Sometimes there were blueprints. Always there were options, photos from previous projects or magazines or Pinterest, for consideration.

For this unexpected session there were only the things from the box. The journal. A fist formed in Anne's chest. The photographs she'd never seen. Knots tightened in her belly. A dozen or more newspaper clippings. A key. Curiosity joined the mix of emotions. She picked up the key and turned it over. No markings, but there was a number stamped into the metal: 168. Could be an apartment key. Maybe a lockbox key. Anne had no idea.

Then there was the necklace. Delicate silver chain with a locket. There were two tiny photos inside. One was of a woman she believed to be

Mary Morton with a young man. The other was even harder to distinguish other than the fact that there appeared to be three women huddled together.

Maybe there was something in the journal about the locket.

The pink blanket... Anne pulled it from the box and smoothed her hand over it. Was this the blanket she'd been wrapped in after she was born? Tiny white flowers dotted the soft pink fabric. She set it aside.

These items represented the life of Mary Morton. A murderer who had died in prison at the age of fifty-two after nearly twenty-nine years served.

The doorbell sounded, and Anne jumped. She pressed her hand to her chest and forced a breath. This whole thing had her far too jumpy. Of all the surprises she had hoped might come into her life, this was not one of them.

She hurried to the door, checked the viewfinder. *Lisa*. When Anne had called her, she'd told her friend first about the business news. Like her, Lisa had been ecstatic. She wanted to celebrate. Then Anne had spilled about the unexpected visitor. Lisa couldn't believe it. On some level, Anne still didn't.

She unlocked the door and wrenched it open. Anne had gotten so caught up in the contents of the box she hadn't realized enough time had passed for Lisa to be here already. "Thanks for coming. This is..." She took a breath. "This is something I just can't do alone."

There were few things Anne had ever felt she wasn't prepared to face alone—God knew she'd had no real choice in the matter—but this... This was different. She really needed an objective voice here.

Rather than immediately respond, Lisa grabbed her in a hug and squeezed. "I'm so sorry this is happening."

For a few seconds Anne sagged into her dear friend's embrace. Then she drew back. "It's okay. I just need to be sure that I make a decision that won't come back to haunt me in the future."

As much as she hated to admit it, Mr. Brenner had been right about that. Mary Morton was dead. Anne wanted to put her and the nightmare legacy behind her. But first, she needed to do this...maybe. The final decision was still up in the air.

Lisa closed the door and locked it. "Of course you do. This is a big deal. It's like if you don't do it, you'll always be wondering. And if you do..." She shrugged. "It's an enormous decision."

Her friend was right, even if Anne didn't want to acknowledge it. If she simply said no without further consideration, she might truly regret the decision in the future. Why not just do this and move on once and for all? Sounded simple enough. Well, maybe not simple, but straightforward.

Doubt nudged her. Or not. One way or the other she had only a few hours to make a decision with which she could live.

"Would you like something to drink?" Anne led the way to the dining table. "I've already had a cocktail, but I could go for another."

Lisa dropped her shoulder bag onto a chair and set her attention on Anne. "Have you had lunch?"

Her friend knew her too well. "I was just about to when that guy arrived." She stared at the items spread across her table. "I forgot all about food after that."

"I'm ordering pizza. Now."

Anne didn't argue. She needed to eat, and she sure didn't need another cocktail. At least not until after she'd eaten. If there ever was one, *this* was definitely a two-or three-cocktail afternoon.

She was supposed to be celebrating this new big deal. Instead she was fretting over the past.

"Okay." Finished with the pizza order, Lisa tossed her phone onto the table, pulled out a chair and settled into it. "Let's see what we have here."

While her friend studied the items from the

box, Anne went up to her office and grabbed the portfolio for her new clients. In spite of all else, she smiled. Not just clients, she amended, but her big-deal clients who were going to make this little firm a household name. At least in the greater Chicago area.

Hopefully.

At the bottom of the stairs, she contemplated her friend. With this new contract, it was time to make the offer she'd been secretly putting together. If her friend accepted, she and Lisa would become partners.

Smiling to herself, Anne made her way back to the dining table. Lisa was studying the newspaper clippings, her face lined in concentration. She was such a great assistant. Always going above and beyond. Anne knew without a doubt that she would make an amazing partner as well.

"She was young," Lisa said without looking up.

"Yeah." Anne sat down at the table. "She'd just finished her master's in education. She was starting her third year of teaching at an elementary school when the murder happened."

Lisa glanced at her. "You look a lot like her." Anne nodded. "I mean, *a lot* like her."

"I know. It used to bother me," she admitted. "But I blocked it from my mind. In fact, I haven't thought about her—really thought about her—in years. It seems surreal that this is happening." She dropped into a chair across the table from Lisa. "I'm still reeling at the shock. I feel torn in a dozen directions. Afraid. Seriously, I feel like a kid who doesn't want to look under the bed."

"Understandable." Lisa placed the newspaper clipping back on the table. "Give me the gist of what happened based on what you actually know."

Anne moistened her lips, took a breath and launched into the story. "Mary Morton met Neil Reed in high school. They'd known each other forever, and they were sweethearts all through senior year and through college—though long distance. Mary went to Wheaton with a major in education, and Neil was a student at Northwestern's Pritzker School of Law. They were only an hour or so apart, but still, it made living together difficult. Neil shared an apartment with three other students while Mary got a small studio apartment without roommates, which allowed them to spend their weekends and holidays together."

Lisa frowned. "How do you know those specifics?"

"When I was nineteen I watched a documentary about them." Anne turned her hands up. "I went through something. Maybe because I was in college and the reality of adulthood had hit me hard. I felt like I needed to know all I could." She surveyed the items on the table. "But to tell you the truth, the only thing I learned was what the police discovered and released to the public. There was quite a bit about the trial but basically nothing after that. No really deep details from before or after, you know. There wasn't a lot of attention on the case—ever. That one low-level documentary was the only thing I ever found, and I can't be sure everything in it was accurate."

Lisa nodded. "I get it." She gestured to the journal. "Anything in there?"

"I don't know. I haven't looked beyond the first page. It's almost like I don't want to look." She smirked. "That maybe I'll find something that changes everything—as if the possibility that nothing I thought I knew was right. I'm not sure I'm adequately prepared for that journey. Pathetic, huh?"

"Not pathetic at all." Lisa studied her for a moment. "Did you ever try to visit her?"

Anne looked away. The answer to that question was maybe the most painful of all. Finally, she turned to her friend. "Yes. During that same time, when I was a sophomore in college. After the documentary. I realized I had so many questions. I wanted to talk to her. To know the truth or at least her side of it. So I went to the prison. But she wouldn't see me." She laughed dryly.

"No matter how many times I went, she wouldn't see me. Eventually I stopped going, and that was when I decided I was never looking back. I told myself Mary Morton was nothing to me and I was nothing to her. End of story."

"That's really awful. My first thought is what mother would deny her only child a few minutes of her time when time was all she had." Lisa shook her head. "But the truth is what I'm getting from you is that you've never heard her side of what happened."

The words shook Anne just a little. "Well, no, I suppose not. I mean, I read all these back then." She indicated the clippings with a sweep of her arm. "And everything else that was available ten years ago online. Like I said, I watched the documentary. But that's it. There was nothing else. She wouldn't talk to me, so what was I supposed to do?"

"You did what you could. The situation is not your fault." Lisa surveyed the items on the table once more. "All right, then. As your best friend, this is my advice, for what it's worth. Read the journal. Get her side of things or whatever she wants you to know from those pages. Then decide if you want to do this thing—for you, not for her. None of this is about her anymore. She's gone. This, Anne, is about you."

The suggestion made almost too much sense.

"That's a good idea." Anne's gaze fixed on the journal. "I can read it tonight and then give him my answer in the morning as promised."

The doorbell rang.

Anne jumped, almost laughed. She rarely had unscheduled visitors. Most of the time appearances at her door were either a client or Lisa. Today she felt like she was living at Grand Central Station.

Lisa stood. "That will be the pizza."

Of course. Right. Anne had entirely forgotten the pizza order.

While Lisa went to the door, Anne gathered the clippings and placed them back in the box. She'd read all those articles on the internet. No need to read them again. The locket and key she decided she might need. She held that one photo of the two of them for a moment, stared at the image of herself as a newborn. Then she studied the vague smile on Mary Morton's face. Anne traced the image with the pad of her thumb. The woman in the photo, nearly five years younger at the time than Anne was now, looked happy and at the same time terrified. Why wouldn't she be the latter? She was facing life in prison, and she'd just given birth to a child.

Mary's parents were dead. She'd been accused of murder, and certainly her friends had turned their backs on her. She'd been alone…

Anne knew that feeling all too well.

"Here we go." Lisa placed the pizza box in the center of the table. The scent of freshly baked dough and cheese and meats wafted from it.

Anne tucked the photograph into the journal, then put both, as well as the locket and key, into the box. "I'll get paper plates."

"And cocktails," Lisa reminded her.

Anne smiled in spite of herself. "Coming up!"

She arranged paper plates on the table. Made sure a roll of paper towels was handy. Then she prepared two more of those lovely strawberry-lemonade cocktails—adding extra vodka this time. For a little while they gorged on pizza and sipped their drinks.

"If I decide to do this," Anne said, a new worry niggling at her, "I can't say for sure if I'll be losing a day or a week, and this is really not a good time to be doing that."

Lisa smiled. "If it's our new big client you're worried about—don't. I can handle things for a few days while you do what you have to do."

Admittedly, the idea was troubling. They had just landed this amazing opportunity, and the thought of suddenly being unavailable was terrifying. Anne couldn't help wondering if her distant past was really worth the risk.

That part was still up in the air.

"I know one hundred percent that I can trust

you to go above and beyond. That's not a question. But, just to make sure we're on the same page, let's go over everything." Anne reached for the portfolio she'd brought down from her office. "Of course, you can call me any time no matter where I am."

Did that mean she had made up her mind already?

The idea had her pulse quickening.

"Going over the details is a good idea," Lisa agreed, drawing her back to the here and now. "We're only human." She grinned. "We can't be perfect all the time."

Anne grinned. "Just most of it."

They grabbed more slices of pizza and continued eating as they discussed the details.

"I'll call the contractors and suppliers," Anne said. "Make sure we're good there and send you an email with the dates they give me."

"I can lay out a schedule and pass it along to all parties," Lisa suggested before biting into the thick-crusted slice of pie.

"Add reminders to our calendar." Anne then took a bit of her own slice.

"Will do." Lisa held up her half empty glass. "To the future."

Anne tapped her glass against it. "The future."

She just hoped it wasn't about to turn into a nightmare.

7:30 p.m.

ANNE HAD TOUCHED base with all the necessary contractors and suppliers, then passed along the results of her conversations to Lisa by phone and via email. There appeared to be no glitches to worry about with scheduling. During the calls to the suppliers, she had ordered the items—like the special floor tile—that required additional lead time.

Now, a fourth cocktail in hand—she never had four cocktails in a single day, but somehow this day called for it—she settled onto the sofa to begin reading the journal.

Deep breath. This is the right decision. She opened the slightly worn cover and stared at her mother's handwriting. Then she sipped her cocktail to wash down the lump that had risen in her throat.

Reading this journal was a necessary journey into whatever had been happening when her mother committed murder—or not. Like the documentary, it would be one-sided. That said, in order to have both sides of the issue she had no choice but to do this.

It was often said that the truth would set you free. Anne had no idea if that was true. Mostly the only thing this particular truth had done for her in the past was to make her a pariah. Kids at school had tortured her. Even foster parents had treated her differently. Some had been afraid of her, while others had decided she was something with which to be toyed, and not in a good way. After all she was the daughter of a monster. Why not treat her like a little monster? She'd been mistreated and abused...but mostly she had been neglected and unloved.

No child should grow up believing he or she was alone and unloved.

But it happened all too often.

Maybe that was why she had never managed a long-term relationship. She hadn't been able to trust anyone to care for her or to love her properly as a child. How could she possibly trust anyone as an adult? The answer was she could not.

She'd had the occasional date. Even an official boyfriend once or twice, but nothing lasted more than a month or two. The first one had only been interested in sex, as were most teenage boys. The other was obsessed with true crime and, as it turned out, only dated her in hopes of learning the dirty details.

Nothing ever lasted.

"Get over it," she muttered. This was her life.

To her credit she had made the most of it, and damn it, she was proud of her accomplishments. Once this unexpected bump in the road was behind her, she wasn't looking back ever again. Forward would be her only direction.

Satisfied that she had made the right decision, she began to read, starting with the *Present Day* note that had been added to page one by taping pink pieces of notepaper on top.

Chapter Four

Journal Entry
Thirty Years Ago

Sorry—this part is the present, but I had already begun by writing *Thirty Years Ago* when I realized I needed to explain, and it's ink so... Oh well. I didn't have a diary or a journal back then—when I was young and in love and pregnant with you. I was far too busy planning my wedding and working to worry about writing anything down. Besides, who worries about the worst-possible situation actually happening at the most unlikely time? Not me apparently. This I now deeply regret. It's the second biggest regret of my life. It would have been so much easier if I'd kept a log of the details. Oh well, hindsight is twenty-twenty, as they say.

Although it has been three decades since these events occurred, I realized just recently that it was necessary for me to put certain parts in writing. I skip around a little, ensuring that I get the most relevant dates and information down. With my recent cancer diagnosis, my time and energy are limited, and in truth, I can't say that I won't go to sleep tonight and not wake up. If I am able to finish, I hope this journal makes it to you. I know I don't deserve your time or your attention, but this isn't for me. This is for *you*. I want you to know the truth so that whatever bad feelings about who you are and where you came from will be alleviated to some degree.

Also, no matter what you believe, I have always loved you. I loved you before you were born, and I love you now. Your father loved you as well. What happened was the sort of nightmare you might see in a movie or read in a book. It was not something I ever dreamed would happen to us. To this day I wonder how it could have happened without at least some sort of warning.

Anyway, I hope you won't be put off or ignore this journal simply because you hate me. Or perhaps you feel nothing for or about me. Please know that I understand. If I were you I would hate me too. But please keep reading. I beg you to keep reading. Find the truth...for *you*.

I'm sure you're likely wondering why now. Why did I wait all this time to contact you in any way? After all, you came to the prison several times, and I refused to see you. That is my first and biggest regret in this life. Once it was clear an appeal was not going to happen, I thought I was doing the right thing by staying out of your life and never allowing you to be part of mine. It was the most difficult decision of my existence. I wanted you to be free of me and the regret and pain I carried. And the stigma, of course. I noticed you changed your name, and I'm glad. You deserve to be free of any connection to the horror that was my final year of freedom.

I'm sure you're laughing as you read. Why wouldn't the murder be my biggest regret? The answer is painfully simple. I did not murder anyone. I swear this to you. I am innocent. I don't expect you to believe me, which is why I have started this journal. When it's done I'm sending all that I have left along with the journal to the Colby Agency. Another inmate told me that the Colby Agency are the best private investigators. Not that she ever used them, but she knows people who know people. I did a little research on the internet, and it seems to be true. In the end, I'm counting on someone at the Colby Agency to find the truth. You see, I don't know who killed the love of my life. Neil's murder, I am confident, was committed by someone close to us. I can tell you the people I believe did this, but I cannot prove anything. My hope is that the Colby Agency can do what I and the police could not. Actually, I'm praying they will. Again, not for me, but for *you*.

Anyway, here goes. Please, please keep reading.

May 5
Thirty Years Ago

I HAD JUST found out I was pregnant. I was so thrilled. I can't even find the words to describe how amazing it felt. I couldn't wait to tell Neil. He was going to be over the moon. Although we had intended to wait until we were a little more settled—at least until after the wedding—to start a family, it didn't matter. This was amazing. And maybe under the circumstances we could forego the bigger wedding his mother had planned and just elope. That would have actually been pretty perfect.

We had been looking at houses with our best friends, Eve Redford and Kevin Langston. Eve and I had known each other since we were children. She met Kevin at a sorority party sophomore year, and they have been a couple since. It was nice that Kevin and Neil hit it off. Eve and I couldn't have been happy unless our future husbands were friends. That's the way best friends were supposed to be, you know. We wanted to do things together…to be friends forever. We had lost the third member of our bestie trio—Carin Carter. She was one of us until she wasn't. I don't know what happened, but one day she just decided we couldn't be friends anymore. She had not spoken to me or to Eve in weeks. We later learned she moved to Chicago and never looked back. Which is all the more reason Eve and I understood we had to stick together. We would never allow anything to come between us. Best friends forever.

Except something did…something unthinkable…something straight out of a horror movie. Something I never saw coming.

SIDE NOTE: YOU SHOULD know that what I felt that long ago May all changed by August of that same year. Eve Redford was not my friend after all. I later wondered if who she really was is the reason Carin left. I can't be sure about that. But what I can say with absolute certainty is that Eve Redford was not who she appeared to be. I imagine she is still that same deceitful person. Did she murder my sweet Neil? I don't know, but I believe she knows who did. Whatever you do, be careful around her. Do not trust her under any circumstances. I have no proof…no evidence whatsoever. But what I can say is that I know in my heart with utter certainty that someone close to me murdered my future husband—your father. I just don't know which of the three—Eve or Kevin or, maybe, Carin.

If I could have figured out the motive maybe I could have uncovered the truth. I can only assume that the evil person who killed him did not want me to continue being happy. There simply is no other explanation. Neil was the kindest, most honorable man I have ever known. No one, and I mean no one, could have found a single thing bad in him that warranted harm, much less murder.

Obviously, the killer didn't want the man I loved because he or she killed him. She didn't want the child I carried. Otherwise he or she would have taken you in under the guise of friendship. I just don't know. The one thing I know with absolute certainty is that you cannot trust those three or anyone close to them. Bottom line: Do not trust anyone who was close to me. And please, please be careful.

Chapter Five

Aurora
Wednesday, July 9
Holiday Inn Express
Broadway Avenue, 9:00 a.m.

Anne sat in her car for a while. She'd been sitting here ten minutes already. When she called Jackson Brenner she told him she would arrive at his hotel at nine. And she was here, but somehow she wasn't ready to get out and do this thing. It was a foolish reaction, but there it was.

He had offered to come to her house, but she'd preferred to do this in neutral territory. For now, she wanted—no, needed—this to be separate from her real life. She was Anne Griffin, a survivor. A college graduate against all odds who had started her own business. A girl who had built something out of nothing.

This...*this* thing from before she was born had no place in her real life, and she intended to keep it that way until she knew more. She had worked far too hard to become her own person—not the child of a murderer—to risk that reputation. Despite those feelings and her determination, on some level she understood that if she didn't do this the mystery and shame of that past would forever follow her like a lost and unwanted shadow. She needed it behind her permanently and irrevocably.

Deep breath.

With effort, she opened the car door and got out. Squaring her shoulders, she elbowed the door closed and tapped the handle to secure it. A soft beep confirmed the vehicle was locked.

Anne strode to the entrance of the hotel and hesitated long enough to draw in another deep, solidifying breath before entering the lobby. She followed a corridor to the elevator and then rode up to the second floor. Heart pounding, she walked along the upstairs corridor until she reached the room number he'd given her. Then she knocked on the door.

This was it. The point of no return.

The slab of stained and polished wood opened instantly as if he'd been standing on the other side waiting for her arrival.

He smiled. "Ms. Griffin, come in."

He stepped away, giving her space. She entered the room and closed the door. She was really doing this. He'd offered to meet her in the lobby or the parking lot, but she had wanted to do this in private. Besides, if she couldn't trust this man in his hotel room she certainly couldn't trust him as a near constant companion for the next day...or few days.

Go big or go home.

She had used that motto throughout her post-college struggle to create her own company. No doubting herself. She could do this. She had to do this. Moving on required this one big step.

"Would you like to sit?" He gestured to the table and chairs that fronted the lone, large window. "Coffee? Anything?"

A carafe and cups, along with two bottles of water, sat on the table.

She walked to the table and sat. "No coffee for me." She did, however, accept a bottle of water. Her throat was bone dry.

"I presume you read the journal?" He eased into a chair at the table, took the other bottle of water.

"I did." She twisted off the cap and had a sip to moisten her throat.

"What's your decision, then?"

"To be honest..." She looked him square in the eyes. He had nice eyes. "I'm still torn. Part of me feels the whole thing is preposterous. But I decided to give your agency the benefit of the doubt. The Colby Agency has a stellar reputation." She had done some deep digging on the agency last night and been duly impressed. "Since you decided to take the case, I'm confident you see something I cannot."

He nodded. "We do."

She held the bottle tighter, considered another swallow. "Please, tell me—what is it that you see?"

His blue eyes searched hers for a moment before he answered. He really did have nice eyes. "Holes. We see holes."

"In the investigation, or in Mary Morton's story?"

He shrugged. "Both, to some degree, but primarily in the investigation. We're of the opinion that your mother was railroaded into the conviction. That said, we can't assure you that she was innocent and wrongly convicted, but we feel there are serious enough questions to doubt her guilt."

Anne's chest tightened. "So you believe this can be proven one way or the other even now... three decades later."

"Yes."

He seemed so certain. How could he be based on the journal that a convicted murderer had written in her final days of life? "I don't see how. I mean, yes, her story does suggest the possibility of other suspects, and certainly she insists on her innocence. But how could the police have gotten it so wrong?"

For a long moment he studied her as if attempting to determine how best to answer her question. After a bit he said, "The police are only human. They make mistakes. Once in a while a member of that upstanding group decides to do something bad. Maybe because he's just not a good guy or maybe for the money. Either way, no unit or agency is exempt from the occasional bad apple or mistake. Then again, the detective who investigated the case was fairly young. The issue may have been nothing more than inexperience."

"He was thirty-two," Anne argued. She wasn't even thirty yet. Thirty-two didn't seem so young to her.

"But he'd only been a detective for two years—that's the issue, in my opinion. He was inexperienced in this sort of investigation."

The idea took her aback. "Are you saying he had never investigated a murder before?"

"He had—twice, in fact. But both were cut-and-dry cases where the evidence was clear and the suspects more than apparent—one even came with a confession. The Reed case was complicated with no clear-cut evidence. There should have been a seasoned detective assigned to the case."

Anne couldn't sit any longer. She stood. Paced

the length of the room. "Then why did her attorney have trouble trying for an appeal? I mean, if the lack of a thorough investigation was so evident, it seems to me an appeal should have been almost automatic."

"The attorney is another bone of contention, in our opinion," Brenner explained. "He was a public defender. Not to say there aren't plenty of great attorneys in a public defender's office, but this one was also really young, with few cases under his belt. Worse, he was overworked—as most are. The circumstances were ripe for failure."

He turned his hands up. "As for appeals, they're granted when there is proof of ineffective counsel, prosecutorial or jury misconduct, or maybe some sort of evidence that was left out or newly discovered evidence—something that suggests the defendant deserves a second chance at proving her innocence. All the attorney or the judge had to do in order to deny an appeal was to say there was no legal standing for appeal— which he did because there was nothing brought to his attention that would suggest otherwise. The attorney should have been helping her find what she needed to persuade the judge."

Anne paused in her pacing and allowed a deeper breath. "What you're saying is that whatever happened, Mary Morton had lost before the investigation and the trial even began?"

"That's what I'm saying."

The notion sat like a load of rocks on her shoulders. "What are the chances you can actually find the truth?" She held up a hand before he could answer. "I'm not asking if you can overturn the verdict. What good would that do at this point? I'm asking if you realistically believe you can uncover what really happened."

He stood, pushed in his chair, then pressed her with his gaze. "If you allow me, I will find the truth. Do not doubt it. The Colby Agency hired me because I have a knack for solving cold cases." He shrugged. "You don't know me, and this is a sensitive situation, so I get why you feel hesitant. But know this—if you allow me to look into the case, I will find the answers. If the truth is what you're looking for, whatever that truth is, I will give it to you when I'm finished."

If she'd had any doubts when she walked into this room, he had satisfied those uncertainties. Whatever else Jackson Brenner was, the man was convincing. "Then let's get this done."

JACK HAD WORRIED when he left Anne Griffin's home yesterday that she wouldn't want to move forward with the investigation. Then, when she'd showed up this morning he had still felt on some level that she wasn't fully convinced it was the right thing to do. Whether he had persuaded her or she'd talked herself into it, he was glad the answer was yes.

This was the kind of case he liked best—one where there was an opportunity to see justice done in an unjust situation.

"Thank you," he said, relieved. "For trusting me."

She gave a vague nod. "What do we do next?"

"I would suggest we take your car back to your place and go to Crystal Lake together. We can discuss the case during the drive."

A frown marred her brow. "I would feel better taking my car."

He got it. Frankly, he would have been surprised if she'd agreed to ride with him, a total stranger. "No problem. We'll drive to Crystal Lake. I've reserved two connecting rooms at the Water's Edge Hotel. Once we're settled in, we'll begin by taking a tour of the area—where Mary Morton and Neil Reed lived. Where their friends lived then and now. Where they worked, past and present."

"We'll get the lay of the land, so to speak," she suggested.

"Yes. After that we'll go over what the agency has found related to the friends your mother—Mary mentioned in the journal."

"We can't do that part now?" Her expression

had taken on a decidedly interested appearance. "I'd really like to know what you've found."

He indicated the table and the chairs they had abandoned. "Why not? Since we're driving separately, it'll give you something to think about en route."

The drive was just over an hour. If she had details to consider hopefully she wouldn't have time to doubt her decision to dive in.

She eased into the chair she'd deserted, and he did the same.

"Coffee?" He'd had two cups already, so he was set.

Anne held up a hand. "I don't think my nerves can handle more caffeine. I had two cups before driving over here."

He smiled. "I'm regretting that second cup I downed as well."

Her face told him she was ready to listen to something beyond small talk. She was even more attractive in person than in the photos he had seen. Her brown hair was long. It swept from a side part and hung around her shoulders. But her eyes were the most flattering asset in his opinion. Deep chocolate brown. Wide and expressive.

"So…" She dragged out the one syllable.

Jack snapped to attention, kicking himself for getting caught up in analyzing her. "So, Mary Morton's best friend, Eve Redford, married the year after the trial. She married Kevin Langston—her boyfriend at the time of Neil Reed's murder. Kevin went on to do the bigger things he touted as his plan back in law school at the University of Chicago—according to interviews I watched from ten years ago. He worked as head legal counsel for one of the top research companies, BioTech, for the first nine years after law school, then he ran for the state senate. He served there for two terms and then ran for the US Senate, which is where he has served since. His wife, Eve, has made a career as a socialite, though she started out as a social worker." He chuckled. "A bit of a turnaround for her. I would say by her many efforts to show up in the papers and on social media that she loves every minute of it."

"What about Carin Carter?" Anne asked. "According to the journal, she parted ways with Mary and Eve before the murder. There was some sort of falling out, I presume."

"She did. The reasons for the parting of ways remains unknown, but Carin left Crystal Lake and married an investor in Chicago. She worked as a secretary in various state government offices, eventually becoming a personal assistant to the Illinois governor at the time. By then her husband had passed away and she'd inherited a small fortune. This is where things start to twist backward a bit. When Kevin Langston got elected to the US Senate, Carin joined him there as a personal assistant. The two have worked together since. If you peruse photos of the Langstons online, you'll find Carin somewhere in the background in most of them. Though none ever show Carin and Eve looking all chummy the way they once did when they were younger."

"I tried searching for Carin online." Anne visibly relaxed as they talked. "I didn't find much of anything."

"That's because she goes by her married name—Wallace. She never used her maiden name for anything relevant to her work in politics, so considering the timing, most everything about her that hit and stuck on the internet as it evolved has always been under the name Wallace. Her life as a Carter was during the internet's infancy, so it's not unusual that you didn't find anything."

"Then those three are back together."

"For the past decade or so, yes."

Anne took a minute to evaluate the information he'd passed along. "What are your thoughts about the three, based on what you know at this point?"

He smiled. "You know the old saying—you don't get far in politics without a few skeletons in your closet. Does that mean that Kevin Langston or his personal assistant, Carin Carter Wallace, is guilty of murder or an accessory to murder? Who knows. It tells me that they're fearless on some level. Not afraid to face negativity or tough battles. They're determined and maybe a little on the ruthless side. As for the wife, Eve, I would say the same. None have had so much as a traffic ticket. Can we be sure they've never done anything illegal because of the lack of negative hits? Not at all. But as for what this indicates relative to our investigation, we're looking at people who are high profile, have some level of loyalty in their community and who have everything to lose."

"We're facing an uphill battle," Anne surmised.

"We are. But all any of this ultimately suggests is that we have no specific thing to look at. No particular time frame beyond that of the murder. Which dictates that we must go back to the beginning and trace these people and what they did, who they did it with and what resulted from their actions until we find what we're looking for. It takes a little longer, but the result is the same."

Anne's slim shoulders sagged. "This may take a while."

He couldn't pretend otherwise. "It's possible that it will take some time, yes. But in my experience, whenever an investigation begins word gets around pretty quickly. Once that happens anyone who has something to hide will get nervous. When people get nervous they make mistakes."

She nodded slowly as understanding sank in. "They do things they might not otherwise do in an effort to protect themselves."

He grinned. "They do. The more nervous they get, the more risks they take, which allows for more noticeable mistakes. That's when we'll start to see whatever one or all are hiding. That," he emphasized, "is when the real story will start to emerge."

A blink, followed by another and then another warned that her emotions were getting the better of her. "I..." She took a moment, then pressed her fingertips to her eyes. "I didn't want to do this." She met his gaze, her dark brown eyes liquid with the mounting emotion. "But after I read the journal, I felt like I had to know in order to get on with my life without this...this nightmarish history hanging around my neck."

He wanted to reach out and squeeze her hand, give her a pat on the shoulder...something to comfort her, but that wouldn't be a good move. He imagined that trust wasn't easily gained with this woman. "I—all of us at the Colby Agency—recognize how difficult this must be for you. In truth, I wrestled with the idea of including you in the investigation. My boss, Victoria, insisted, but I wasn't so sure it was the right thing to do."

Anne searched his face, hers uncertain. "What changed your mind?"

"The more I looked at the case as a whole, I realized something important. As much as Mary Morton wanted the truth to come out—as insistent as she was that she was innocent—this really was never about her. She had accepted her fate. Which is why she stopped fighting the appeals process. It's why she refused to see you when you became of age. She didn't want you to live the rest of your life with this thing hovering in the background like a dark cloud ready to rain on you at the worst possible time."

Anne visibly held her breath…waited for him to go on.

He shook his head, dead certain in his assessment. "As time went on she recognized that there was only one way to make this right. Then she learned of the cancer and that her time was short and she grew desperate, which is why she contacted the agency. But this was not about her. She confirmed as much in her journal. This is, and always has been, about *you*."

The mixture of emotions on Anne's face spoke loudly and clearly of her understanding. She got it, and she appeared prepared to do this for herself and maybe even for her mother.

Chapter Six

Johnsburg
Water's Edge Hotel
Chapel Hill Road, Noon

The rooms were on the second floor and had balconies that overlooked the water. Not such a bad way to spend the next few days. The community of Johnsburg was one of many smaller ones that surrounded Crystal Lake.

Anne wandered from the closed sliding door that led onto the balcony back to the queen-size bed that stood in the center of the room. She opened the small suitcase she had tossed there. She had packed for a stay through the weekend. Being home by Monday was, in her mind, a hard deadline.

Not that she couldn't nudge it deeper into next week if necessary, but she preferred to be home by then. Since going out on her own she had never spent more than a day or two from work. Lisa would handle things. No need, really, to worry about the business, but somehow she couldn't help herself.

Jackson Brenner had been right, she realized. He'd given her a lot to think about on the drive here. It hadn't taken that long. Just over an hour. She'd spent that time wondering why none of her mother's supposed closest friends had checked on Anne after she was moved into foster care. She imagined it was possible one or the other had attempted to take her in and had been turned down. Anne couldn't see any reason that would have happened. The more likely scenario was that no one had tried. None testified on Mary's behalf. Given their testimony, why in the world would any have wanted to welcome her child into their lives? Eve Redford (now Langston) and Kevin Langston had been called as defense witnesses, but their testimony had been damaging rather than helpful. Carin Carter, now Wallace, had been out of the picture by then.

Was the lack of support from close friends because Mary had been guilty?

Apparently so—in their minds anyway.

Anne pushed the thoughts away for the moment and removed the clothes from her bag. She hung up the tees and jeans along with the two more businesslike blouses she had added at the last moment. One pair of dress pants and two pairs of jeans. She'd worn her favorite sneakers and packed a pair of leather loafers to go with the dressier attire.

Her cosmetics bag she stored in the bathroom. Not that she wore that much makeup. Mascara and a very basic foundation. Occasionally she added a little blush, so she'd brought that too. Makeup and nail polish weren't her things. She preferred simple and easy to maintain. A hairbrush and deodorant along with a toothbrush and paste were necessary.

The skin lotion she used at night was her only fragrance. And it was so subtle no one ever noticed it.

But that was Anne. Simple. Basic. Rarely noticed beyond her design skills.

She thought of the man in the next room. He was tall, broad shouldered. Very nice eyes. They were kind, expressive. He had a nice smile too. Most important, he seemed really good at his work. She supposed the next few days would tell the tale on that one. She had no reason to expect otherwise given that the Colby Agency had such a prestigious reputation. She'd actually been surprised at what a big deal the agency was. The fact that they had taken up her mother's case was almost shocking. Anne felt confident it wasn't for any sort of accolades—and certainly not for money.

Maybe it was because they liked championing the underdog.

A soft knock on the door drew her in that direction. She checked the viewfinder. Her partner for this endeavor. *Time to get this show started.* She took a deep breath and opened the door. "Let me grab my purse and I'm ready."

"Lunch first, or straight into the tour?"

Brenner waited in the door while she grabbed her shoulder bag from the desk. Her stomach said eat, but her brain wanted to get on with what they'd come to do. Her brain generally won out in these sorts of debates, which was why Lisa was constantly after her about forgetting to eat.

"If it's okay," she said as she approached the door once more, "we can start the tour and eat a little later."

"Absolutely." He held up a hand, two protein bars fisted there. "I thought you might say that."

She accepted one of the bars. "Thank you." She opened the wrapper as they walked to the stairs. Her stomach had decided to remind her that she actually was hungry.

By the time they reached the lobby she had scarfed down the bar. Brenner grabbed a couple of bottles of water from the machine in the niche near the exit and tossed one to her. Funny how quickly she was beginning to really like this guy.

In the lot he opened the passenger-side door of

his car and waited for her to climb in. Once he'd closed the door and settled behind the steering wheel she asked, "What should I call you? Do you prefer Mr. Brenner or Jackson?"

Seemed like she would have asked or he would have said before now. But it had been a strange twenty odd hours. Maybe he had and she'd simply forgotten.

"Most people call me Jack," he said as he backed out of the parking slot.

"Jack it is, then." She watched as he navigated from the lot and onto the road. "Everyone calls me Anne. My name is actually Marianne but I've never gone by that."

"So, Anne." He glanced at her, smiled. "What made you decide to keep your first name when you changed your last name?"

She considered the question and the passing landscape as he drove. "It was the last name and all the baggage it carried that I wanted to get away from. The other didn't seem relevant at the time."

"You could have used your father's last name."

A valid point. "The newspapers and online articles all quoted Mary's friends as saying that Neil Reed was her longtime boyfriend and future husband and, of course, my father, but he wasn't named on the birth certificate. I don't know if it was an error due to the circumstances." She shrugged. "I mean, being born in a prison isn't exactly an ideal situation. But, in the end, I opted for something completely different. I read a book once with a character named Anne Griffin and…" She shrugged. "I guess it stuck with me and it certainly took me out of the situation altogether."

"I get that." He flashed her a smile as he turned onto Big Hollow Road. "I'm sure, as you say, the birth certificate was an error. Mary never deviated in her certainty that Neil Reed was your father."

"No one else questioned it either, to my knowledge. I've always assumed that made it true." She turned her attention to the landscape then. They were nearly *there*…to the place where her parents had lived before disaster struck.

Mostly trees and houses dotted both sides of the road until they reached the little town of Round Lake. Johnsburg, Round Lake—they were all bedroom communities near Crystal Lake. All within a few minutes driving distance of each other.

He made the turn onto Washington Street and then onto Fairlawn Drive before he started to slow. "This is the place."

If they had turned in the opposite direction on Washington Street, Fairlawn would have taken them to the waterfront homes on Lake Shore Drive.

But this was no waterfront home, and it was nothing like Lake Shore Drive.

This was a little house built eighty or more years ago. It looked like a rehab special that no one had decided to tear down but obviously should have. The narrow lot was overgrown. It was easy to see why anyone would just pass it by and never consider a rehab or rebuild.

This was where the woman who had given birth to her had lived when her life went to hell in the proverbial handbasket.

"Wow. Looks as if no one has lived here in decades." A real dump. The photo from the newspaper back then hadn't shown it this way. It had been a neat little cottage surrounded by blooming flowers and mature trees. The tiny lawn had been well kept. The paint hadn't been peeling.

"I spoke to a clerk in the property office," Jack told her, "and she says the place was and still is owned by Neil Reed's father. They've sent warnings about the condition of the property, but he never does anything. Just last week they labeled it condemned."

"Why haven't they razed it? Don't cities do that in extreme cases where owners refuse to take the proper action?" In her line of work, she had heard about those sorts of situations, especially in neighborhoods being gentrified. Or under consideration for gentrification. Failure to pay taxes and/or to properly maintain a property often resulted in the city taking action—sometimes extreme action.

"Apparently," Jack explained, "Preston Reed, Neil's father—your grandfather—has an in with someone on the city's hierarchy and action is never taken. This isn't the first time it's been listed as condemned and then later removed from that status. I suppose Mr. Reed has his reasons for wanting to leave it as is."

Grandfather. At some point Anne had read that her purported biological father had a living father. But she had assumed since he hadn't taken her in as an infant that he wanted nothing to do with her either.

She stared at the house where Mary had lived the last two years of her freedom. There was no reason to believe that because Mr. Reed had kept his son's home for all those years that he cared one iota for his grandchild. Hanging on to the house might've only been related to it being the last place where his son lived. As for why he would ignore Anne, maybe he had reason to believe Mary had cheated on Neil. If she murdered him, she was certainly capable of other atrocities.

Anne dismissed the thoughts. Really, she had

no idea what sort of people her biological mother and father and grandparents were.

Jack pulled into the drive—a strip of lesser overgrowth rendering the driveway very nearly hidden.

"Are we going in?" She instinctively leaned forward. The possibility suddenly had her heart beating faster. Her palms itched with anticipation.

"Might not be safe to go inside, but we can look through the windows and make that determination. The clerk said whatever we do, they are not responsible for any injuries we might sustain since it is listed as condemned. Not to mention, there's always the trespassing and breaking-and-entering charges if we're caught."

Anne felt giddy suddenly. "I'm willing to take the risk if you are. I would really like to go inside if possible." Especially if no one else had lived in the house in all these years. On some level she recognized this was a bit on the foolish side. What difference did where they lived make? Why take such a risk?

What was she even doing here, really?

Just stop. She ordered the dissenting voice away. She had to do this. Had to know as much as possible…to understand before she could put the past fully behind her. After reading that journal Mary had written, there was no way for

Anne to pretend she no longer cared. The disinterest she had feigned all these years had been a lie she told herself so she wouldn't look back. No more lying to herself.

Jack shut off the engine. "We'll have a look and go from there." He gave her a nod and got out.

"Works for me."

Moving quickly, she did the same before he could hustle around to open her door. She joined him at the front of the car. A long survey of the small yard had her thankful she'd worn her sneakers and jeans. Gardening boots would have been better, but at least she wasn't wearing sandals or high heels.

He walked ahead of her, threading his way through the massive shrubs to follow the barely visible brick walk that led to the porch steps. The scrape of branches had her wishing she'd chosen a long-sleeved blouse too, no matter that the temperature was well into the eighties. She frowned at the condition of the porch and steps. Both looked less than reliable.

With a careful step onto the first tread and then the next, Jack tested the steps. When he reached the porch, he gave her a nod. "So far, so good."

She followed the path he'd taken. The porch itself was missing a board or two, but the section that led to the front door felt sound enough. No creaking or bouncing. At the door he gave the knob a twist, but it was locked. Anne's hopes deflated.

"Wait." She thought of the key in the box of personal items. "What was the house number?"

He met her gaze, grinned as if the same thought had just occurred to him as well. "168. I'll get that key."

She'd brought the box along, not wanting to leave it in the hotel room. As foolish as it might've sounded considering there really was nothing of true value inside, she hadn't wanted to risk it disappearing.

Maybe it was a little paranoid to be afraid to leave it, but now she was glad she'd made the decision. She was also very grateful that Jack Brenner was such a gentleman.

Jack returned with the key, the steps creaking this time. "Here goes nothing." He inserted it into the lock. The door opened.

Anne gave a nod. "We didn't have to do any breaking and entering after all."

"Feels like an arguable point if we're caught."

She liked this man more all the time.

Inside was dark considering that trees and bushes surrounded the place as if preparing to swallow it up. Any sunlight that might have been afforded by the windows was effectively blocked. Anne tried a switch, but no light came on.

"And—" there was a clicking sound followed by a beam of light "—I grabbed the flashlight from the glove box."

"I'm glad one of us came prepared." Anne hadn't even considered the possibilities of what they would find, much less what they would need at this house. Based on how many houses requiring rehab she'd been inside, she, of all people, should have thought of a flashlight if nothing else. The flashlight apps on phones were great in a pinch but not quite as good as the original thing.

The front door entered directly into the living room. An old sofa still remained in the middle of the room, along with an end table and coffee table. There was an old-fashioned cabinet-style television. No rug or other pieces.

Anne stared at the floor in the center of the room, her heart pounding once more. That spot was where Neil Reed had fallen...had died. The rug she'd seen in the one photo of the place was, she supposed, why there was no blood soaked into the wood. The rug had been amid the photos of the crime scene in one or more articles she'd read. Now the only thing on the wood floor was decades of dust. She blinked and turned away.

The smell of grime and that closed-up odor assaulted her senses as if she'd just awakened from a deep sleep and found herself in this unknown place.

Wood floors...white walls adorned with cobwebs in every corner. No crown molding. Dark-stained wood baseboards, door and window trim. A number of framed photographs hung on the wall. The one that drew Anne was an eight-by-ten of Mary Morton and Neil Reed. Their smiling faces and the way they embraced each other while staring at the camera made Anne's breath catch. They looked so young. And very much in love. Anne wondered when the photograph had been taken. Compared to the ones she had seen of the two in the newspaper clippings and online, this was likely taken months or perhaps a year before the murder.

But none of those details were responsible for her pulse suddenly racing faster with each breath. It was the realization of how very much she looked like Mary. They had the same color hair and eyes. But the online and newspaper images had not shown so shockingly clear how closely Anne's facial features resembled Mary's. They were like twins.

Anne drew in a steadying breath and moved on.

To the left of the front door was a short hallway with three doors lining it. To the right was the living room and the kitchen. No separate dining room. She decided on the hallway to the left and that first door, which led into a bedroom. She tried the switch. Same as in the living room—no light. The power had likely long ago been disconnected.

There was a bed, covers straightened, pillows arranged at the headboard as if someone had just made the bed and hurried away to work. Except the covers were laden with dust and what appeared to be rat feces. She stood in the middle of the room, took out her phone and turned on the flashlight app so she wasn't tethered to Jack. She could follow her instincts rather than just tagging along after him. Dust and swags of cobwebs layered the once-white walls and barewood floors just as in the living room. Wherever she stepped, a shoeprint was left behind in the thick dust. The bed was a double, small by today's standards for a couple.

There was a dresser with a mirror, both covered with dust as well. Anne wandered in that direction. An empty bottle of perfume stood amid the grime, its label worn by time and use. Anne picked it up and sniffed the pump-sprayer head. Had Mary worn this perfume daily or just on special occasions? The idea that she had touched this perfume bottle shivered through Anne. She set the bottle aside and checked the drawers. All but one was empty save for more dust and a mud-dauber nest. The one drawer contained men's socks and underwear.

The only thing hanging on the wall besides cobwebs was a floral painting above the bed. The closet was empty of female belongings, but there was a suit and a few men's shirts hanging on one end. Neil Reed's, Anne imagined. She slid her fingers along the sleeve. A pair of men's loafers sat on the floor. Like everywhere else, years of disuse and neglect covered the items like a layer of fine, brownish snow.

Why had these things been left here and others taken away? It was almost like a shrine to the murder victim. Then she understood. This was the last place the owner's—supposedly her grandfather's—son had lived, and Mr. Reed couldn't bring himself to change or do away with his belongings. Of course, that was assuming he was a nice and sentimental person.

Anne had her doubts considering he never bothered to check on her.

Jack caught up with her, and they moved on to the next door in the narrow little hall. It was a second, even smaller bedroom that held a desk and bookcases. Ungraded school papers lay on top of the desk. Jack went through the three drawers in the desk while Anne checked the tiny closet. The door had been turned into a makeshift bulletin board complete with corkboard. A couple of school notices were posted there, the pages yellowed and the corners curled. A business card from a local law firm had been pinned near the top. If Anne recalled correctly it was the firm where Neil had interned during his final year of law school.

Jack reached down and closed the final drawer of the desk. "Nothing beyond more school papers and supplies in here. I didn't see anything that belonged to Neil."

Anne scanned the books on the shelves. "Apparently Mary was fond of romance novels." One entire shelf was lined with the paperbacks. Another held books on education and teachers' manuals.

Jack joined her. "My mother is a huge fan of romance novels." He sent her a sideways glance. "How about you?"

"Sadly, there is never enough time in the day for me to indulge in reading."

"You should make time for yourself."

With that profound statement, he moved on to the next room. Anne followed, pondering the idea that maybe he was right.

The one bathroom was miniscule. Typical three-piece, sink, tub and toilet, and seriously dusty. Shampoo and soap as well as a razor and aftershave remained.

The kitchen was another small space, shoehorned between the side of the house that was bedrooms and the larger room up front that was the living room. Jack looked through the cabinets and in the fridge and oven. The man was thorough for sure.

Anne lingered at the fridge and studied the small photos peppering the surface. Most were held against the appliance with magnets of various shapes and colors. One magnet was a back-to-school shout-out. Another was an apple with a pencil next to it. But it was the photos that tugged at her senses.

Another smaller version of the eight-by-ten on the wall in the living room. Other candid shots of Mary with her friends. Anne recognized Eve and Carin in two of the photos. Their faces and hairstyles were the same as the photo in the locket. Anne decided those were going with her. One by one she removed the photos from beneath the magnets. She tucked them into her shoulder bag. When they interviewed Mr. Reed, she would offer them to the man. If he didn't seem to care about them, Anne would keep them. Surely he cared since the house remained standing. But if he didn't take action eventually, the house would likely be torn down. Maybe that was his intention after all this time.

Putting thoughts of him out of her mind, she considered all that she had seen. Overall, she imagined that thirty or more years ago the little house would have been considered a nice starter home. Good bones and all the necessary options. But now, like the rest of Mary Morton's existence, it was disintegrating. The thought made Anne sad on some level beyond her control. No matter that she hadn't known the woman... Mary had been her mother.

From there they locked the front door and went out the back. The stoop and its two steps were far ricketier than the front porch and steps. There wasn't a lot to see out back beyond the thick greenery and knee-deep grass. Jack cut through the heavy overgrowth and went inside the detached shed-style garage. It wasn't large enough for today's SUVs or trucks. Absolutely tiny by today's standards.

He came out swiping at a spiderweb he'd walked through.

"Anything?" Anne already knew the answer.

He shook his head.

She turned and stared at the house once more. This was where the couple had, from all accounts, been happy. No one had seen the trouble coming—according to the documentary she had watched. Had Mary hurried home to this place each day after school to prepare dinner for her soon-to-be husband? Had they made love on that double bed and conceived a child in that same room? It would seem so.

But then, if this was home to the fairy tale, what went wrong?

Why shoot and kill the man she loved? The father of her child?

Unfortunately, it was very possible that Anne would never know the answers to those questions. But she intended to give it this one shot. Her gaze lit on Jack. He had insisted he could find the answers.

Would those answers be the ones she wanted to hear?

Anne shook her head. Funny, the end result suddenly mattered in a way she hadn't anticipated.

Chapter Seven

Crystal Lake
Judith's Cocktail Lounge
Williams Street, 2:30 p.m.

Judith's Cocktail Lounge was quite an upscale place, with soft music playing from hidden speakers and tables tucked in cozy niches as well as a bar that offered more seating. The elegant menu offered "small plates" of international appetizers and entrees that smelled as wonderful as they looked. The accompanying menu photos showed the entrees artistically arranged on pure white plates. As a designer, Anne appreciated the pleasing visuals.

She had not realized she was starving until the charcuterie board for two was placed on the table. Once she started eating, any talk had to wait. By the time the wooden board was bare, Anne was utterly stuffed. She sipped her lemon water and finally allowed her mind to replay the tour through the cottage on Fairlawn Drive.

She reached into her bag and pulled out the photos she'd taken from the fridge door. After pushing the board aside, she spread the photos in front of her like a deck of tarot cards. Somehow the images in the photos were every bit as ominous. She tapped the one photo that showed all three of the female friends. "This is the same photo that's in the locket."

Jack nodded. Then he flashed Anne a wide grin. "Look around. That was taken here." He pointed to the elegant bar. "Right there."

She looked from the bar to the photo and nodded. "You're right. Is that why you suggested this place?" She studied the photo again and then surveyed the intimate cocktail bar with new interest.

Jack followed her gaze, taking in the details as well. "It is. The place had a different name then." He shifted his attention to Anne. "She mentioned—in the journal—coming here once a week after school for a girls' night out."

Anne hadn't made the connection considering the new name. "With the headline change," she pointed out, "it's likely under new ownership."

Before he could comment, the waitress paused at their table. "Would you care for a cocktail or coffee?"

Anne smiled. "I'm good—thank you."

"This place has a new name," Jack said when the waitress's attention swung to him, then he gifted her with a charming smile that clearly dazzled her. "Has the management or owner changed as well?"

The waitress, Cherry, returned the smile with a dreamy one of her own. "It used to be JJ's," she confirmed. "For Jerry and Judith Trenton, but the owners got divorced. The wife ended up with the bar in the settlement, and she changed the name to Judith's."

"Is Judith here by any chance?" Anne mentally crossed her fingers.

Cherry, who couldn't have been more than twenty-two or-three, nodded eagerly. "She is. Wednesdays are ladies' poker night, and she's setting up the club room."

"We'd love to say hello," Anne said hopefully. "My mother used to come here. She told me all about the place."

Cherry nodded. "I'll let her know you're here." She looked to Jack once more. "Would you like anything else?"

"No, thanks."

When the waitress had hurried away, Jack gave Anne a thumbs-up. "Good move."

"It's mostly true." She sipped her water. "Like you said, the journal mentioned this place."

"When we leave, we'll drive by the address where the Langstons lived then and now. You won't believe the change—talk about moving up. The apartment building where Carin Carter Wallace lived is gone. There's a huge supermarket there now. Like the Langstons, based on her current address, she's moved way up as well."

"Rumor is," Anne pointed out, "there's money to be made in the world of politics."

Jack chuckled. "There is that."

A gasp drew their attention to the woman suddenly standing next to their table. She looked to be in her late sixties or early seventies. Her white hair was arranged in a youthful bob around an unexpectedly smooth complexion. Her pantsuit was silk and a spectacular blue that emphasized the color of her eyes.

Judith, no doubt. Anticipation and no small dash of anxiety swelled inside Anne.

"Oh my God," the older woman murmured. "You are the spitting image of your mother."

Anne flinched, couldn't help herself. She recovered quickly and held out her hand. "Anne. The long-lost daughter."

Judith shook her hand but then placed her own against her chest. "It's utterly uncanny."

"And you're Judith," Anne suggested.

"I am indeed."

Jack scooted over, making room on his side of the booth. "Please, join us."

The older lady settled into the seat next to him. She smiled at him, her shiny pink lips parting to show off straight, white teeth. "Thank you. And you are..."

"Jack." He offered his hand then. "Jack Brenner from the Colby Agency. I'm helping Anne find the answers she needs."

Her hand fell away from Jack's, and another gasp hissed across her lips. She put her fingers there as if needing to hold back whatever might have popped out next. When her hand dropped to the table, she looked from Jack to Anne. "You're here because we're closing in on the thirtieth anniversary, and you want the whole story."

Anne nodded, going along with the narrative Jack had opened. "I felt it was time."

"Oh, and Mary just passed." Judith made a sad face and shook her head. "Such a tragic story."

"Mary left me her journal and other evidence." Anne stretched the facts just a little. "We're going through everything piece by piece."

Judith's jaw fell open for a moment before she snapped it closed once more. "Things are going to hit the fan, aren't they?"

The twinkle in her eyes told Anne she wasn't sad or angry about the notion.

"Possibly. The truth deserves to be told. In fact—" she turned to Jack "—we were just talking about paying a visit to the Langstons and to Carin Carter Wallace."

That twinkle brightened, and the older woman's grin widened. "This is going to be epic." She nodded sagely. "Finding the whole truth should have happened ages ago."

Anne couldn't help but laugh. Her heart rate had finally started to slow, and she was feeling a little elated. "Any help you can provide with our efforts will be greatly appreciated."

"Well—." Judith nodded "—I'm more than happy to do so." She glanced at Jack. "I'm not a big fan of our illustrious senator and his wife—or his assistant. That said, I was going through a divorce at the time of the murder, so I wasn't with it and available as much as I might have otherwise been."

She turned fully to Anne then. "Mary was here every week with her friends. They had dinner and cocktails. Oh, and they laughed." She sighed, her expression melancholy. "I just don't understand what happened. Mary loved Neil so much. They came by nearly every weekend and had a cocktail, usually on Saturday evenings before going out to dinner. They always made it a point to say hello if I was here. I just can't believe…" She shook her head and fell silent.

Anne's heart was racing again.

Jack leaned in close to Judith. "Don't worry—we're going to find the truth."

Judith smiled at him again. "I cannot wait to watch the fireworks."

A HALF HOUR LATER, they left the bar. Anne drew in a lungful of air as they walked side by side to his car. Her heart rate had only just fallen back down to normal. Not for a moment had she expected to be so moved...so absorbed in this journey.

"You were amazing back there." Jack sent her a sideways look. "Talk about getting the grapevine stirred up. I'm certain, as Judith said, fireworks will follow."

Anne waited while he opened her door. "I don't know what got into me. I felt like Miss Marple. I just couldn't slow the momentum."

She settled into the passenger seat and realized she could not wait to tell Lisa all about the day. As much doubt and uncertainty as she had suffered at the idea of doing this...she was so very glad she'd agreed. There was something here...something that had been rotting away for thirty years...decaying bit by bit. Anne intended to find it before it disappeared completely.

Jack slid behind the steering wheel. "You should watch out. The Colby Agency will be trying to recruit you."

Anne laughed, and for the first time in too long to remember, it felt deep and real and relaxed.

Maybe this had been a really good idea.

Truly, how was she supposed to move on with her life without settling the past once and for all?

This effort really was essential to her future.

FROM THE OUTER limits of Crystal Lake where they did a drive-by of the vintage, aka rundown, apartment building where twenty-and thirty-somethings Eve and Kevin had lived, they drove the twenty minutes to Barrington. Senator Kevin Langton and his wife, Eve, currently lived in a fifteen-thousand-square-foot mansion on Plum Tree Road, recently valued at nearly six million dollars. The place looked more like a castle than a home. Although the property was not on the market, there was a listing on Zillow that showed that the estate included a vast thirty-seven acres. There were walking trails and a barn for horses. The lavish details went on and on.

"This is—" Anne stared at the towering gate that fronted the drive leading to the property "—crazy luxurious."

"Ready to see where the assistant lives?"

Anne had a feeling Carin Carter Wallace's rise from an administrative assistant in a small-town mayor's office to where she was now would be equally astonishing. "I can't wait."

"Like I said, the apartment building was replaced with a big super store," he reminded her. "For perspective, the images of the building before demolition were very much like the one where the senator and his wife once lived."

"I'm amazed at the amount of research you did." His work put hers to shame.

He glanced at her. "Just doing my job."

And Anne was pleased that he'd been so very thorough. It hit her then that they really did have a shot at finding the truth.

The drive was only a couple of minutes from Plum Tree Road and onto Rolling Hills Drive in the same high-end community.

Carin Carter Wallace, the senator's assistant, lived in a far more modern residence consisting of a mere six thousand square feet ensconced on an intimate five acres, valued at just over four million, according to Zillow.

Soaring windows sat in a cutting-edge contemporary design. This home, too, was fronted by a towering gate. Anne wondered if their secrets made them yearn for extra security. But that was petty of her. She didn't know these people.

"Not too shabby," Jack commented.

"One of my foster mothers used to say, 'Pretty is as pretty does.' Maybe we'll find out if all this is representative of what's in their hearts."

Anne had never been one to judge a book by its cover, but something about these people felt very wrong even if she didn't know them. Maybe it was the journal and all that it insinuated. But those words could be nothing more than Mary's bitterness. Time would tell, Anne supposed.

The drive back to the hotel gave Anne time

to do a good deal of thinking. The journal suggested that someone close to Mary and Neil was responsible for the murder. At the moment, the big question in Anne's mind was, Did the astonishing transformation in the lives of those close to Mary and Neil have anything to do with the murder?

Frankly she couldn't see how at this point. But what she could see was the possibility of people who were ambitious, ruthless...maybe capable of anything and who perhaps knew more than they'd told the police. But did that make one or all a murderer? No...but it certainly merited further consideration.

On the other hand, it was very possible these suspicions were popping into her head because those were the things she wanted to see. Was she superimposing their extravagant personal gains onto a scenario of evil that was actually only a theory?

This was personal for Anne—more personal than she would ever have believed. As hard as she might try, remaining completely objective was likely impossible. Though she'd had no relationship with her parents, there was the potential for wanting some tiny aspect of their story to not be a heinous murder story.

All the more reason to be grateful for the Colby Agency's involvement. Jack would keep her grounded and on the right track. He would be objective as it became more and more clear that she might not be able to.

Anne was exhausted when they reached the hotel. At her door she turned to Jack. "Thank you. I'll be honest—I had major reservations about doing this...all the way up until this morning actually. But now, just talking to someone like Judith and seeing where Mary and Neil lived, I can truthfully say that I'm glad I came."

He smiled. "I'm glad too." His gaze was direct when he started to speak once more. "But fair warning—don't thank me until we're done. The part that comes next may not be nearly as much fun."

Anne wasn't put off by his warning. Not yet anyway.

Chapter Eight

Barrington
Thursday, July 10
Langston Residence
Plum Tree Road, 9:30 a.m.

Jack parked down the block from the turn onto the Langston property. He checked his cell since there had been a couple of vibrations during the drive over. The two waiting text messages made him smile. One was from his contact at the Mayo Clinic, the other from Jamie Colby. Each wanted to ensure he'd received the latest information sent to his email.

Having the power of the Colby Agency as backup was the best. He glanced at the woman in the passenger seat. He wondered if she understood yet how lucky she was that her mother had chosen the Colby Agency.

"Did you have a chance to look over the information I sent you?" He turned his attention to Anne.

They'd had breakfast in their respective rooms, so they hadn't really talked this morning. On the drive here she'd been focused on a call from her assistant about an in-progress project.

But now, before knocking on this door and kicking off the day with a serious bang, they needed to talk.

"I did." She stared toward the property that was their destination. "The Langstons made an investment in the research company, BioTech, where the senator worked the first decade of his law career. As he left the company to start his political career, the stocks soared, making them multimillionaires when they sold out. It would seem they have a legitimate explanation for their super lifestyle change."

He was surprised she hadn't made the connection that came with the rest of the information he'd sent her via email. "Maybe you didn't notice that Carin Carter Wallace's husband was an angel investor in BioTech well before she met him...well before the Langstons invested."

She frowned. "So Carin's husband was one of the original investors."

"He was." Jack grinned. "Just one year after his investment in a fledgling company, she shows up in his life and they end up married."

Anne bobbed her head slowly. "Okay, but what's the connection to my parents?"

Surprised didn't begin to cover his reaction to her use of the term *parents*. This was the first time he'd heard her refer to Mary Morton and Neil Reed as parents...out loud anyway. He suspected it was her first time period. He hoped what they found during this investigation didn't make her regret that development.

"I can't confirm anything with any degree of certainty," he said honestly. "But Carin disappeared from the Crystal Lake area and appeared in Wallace's orbit just a couple of months before Neil's murder."

Anne nodded slowly, as if trying to make the connection he meant, then surprise flared in her expression. "Kevin, Eve and Carin were all trying to get involved with this BioTech. With that in mind, maybe Carin didn't just get mad and leave. She may have left with an agenda—to weave her way into Wallace's life."

"Right. And FYI, BioTech got its start right here in Chicago by a young med student, Michael Smith, at Northwestern's Feinberg School of Medicine."

Her eyes widened. "Neil was at Northwestern."

Jack held up his cell. "One of my sources who attended Northwestern just confirmed that the two were friends. But the really interesting part is that Michael Smith and Neil Reed were two of four who shared an apartment for a while."

"Are you serious?"

He nodded. "I am." Even Jack had found this news particularly exciting.

"Wow." She took a breath. "I can see how this company—BioTech—is a definite connection of some sort." She bit her lip, confusion replacing the other emotions that had danced across her face. "But how did that lead to murder?"

"That's what we intend to find out. I can't say for sure this is the connection—*the thread*—that led to murder. But it's one that wasn't explored in the investigation." He shifted back into Drive. "And money matters have long been motives for murder."

"True. But Neil was a law student. The only money matters he had at the time was the mounting debt."

"Still—" Jack braked for the turn into the imposing driveway "—it's a starting place for our search."

"It is a starting place. The fact that all the players except Mary and Neil wound up a part of BioTech does seem a little suspicious."

"Definitely a little suspicious considering that Mary mentioned a new start-up business that wanted Neil on board."

Anne's eyes widened. "You're right. If it was BioTech, then that's a thread that binds them all."

He nodded. "Exactly."

Jack braked again at the gate and powered down his window. Now, if they were lucky, Mrs. Langston was home. He pressed the button on the intercom.

"Good morning," a female voice said. "Please state your name and business."

"Jackson Brenner with the Colby Agency and my colleague, Anne Griffin." He glanced at her. "We're here to see Eve Redford Langston."

He used the woman's maiden name as well to suggest some knowledge of her prior to becoming the senator's wife.

Anne's eyebrows lifted in question. Likely the same question he had. Would the lady of the house allow them into her domain? Would she dare satisfy her curiosity as to why the daughter of Mary Morton was at her gate? He had no doubt the Langstons had already heard the news. Judith Hudson, owner of Judith's, had photos with her lifelong friend, Eve Langston, all over her social media pages. Jack had spent some time perusing those pages last night. The woman no doubt called Langston the instant they left her establishment.

"One moment please."

The seconds ticked off, but neither spoke

while they waited. The pulse at the base of Anne's throat fluttered rapidly. She was nervous…anxious. Who wouldn't be? This was her life—well, her history anyway. Like anyone else, she wanted to understand…to clear up the mystery. He couldn't imagine growing up and finding his way through this world without the strong foundation of his personal history…without the love of his parents and siblings.

So much of Anne's was unknown. Hung in the balance of multiple unanswered questions. And that didn't even take into account the murder.

The gate suddenly started a slow swing inward.

He and Anne exchanged a look. Evidently they were in. The smile that stretched across her face no doubt mirrored his own.

"Drive forward," the seemingly disembodied voice directed. "Park near the fountain and approach the front door."

"Will do." He powered the window up and rolled forward. "We're in."

Anne exhaled a big breath. "She didn't say Eve wasn't in."

"She did not. I'm guessing Eve intends to see us, otherwise why allow the visit to her home?"

"I'm sure the Colby Agency name was persuasive."

"Possibly."

The name often got him through doors he might not have been able to enter. But he suspected Eve Redford Langston knew exactly who Anne Griffin was and why she was here. If Anne hadn't decided Judith had given them up, he'd let her have that one for a bit longer. Judith had pretended to be such a good friend of Mary's. He had a feeling Anne preferred giving people the benefit of the doubt. Surprising in light of the childhood she'd lived.

She was a nice person, he decided. Maybe too nice.

Jack parked on the cobblestone drive that circled a massive fountain which looked exactly like something one might come across in Italy. He exited the car and moved toward Anne's door.

She emerged, staring at the fountain, then the monstrosity of a house with its grand turret. "This is just too much," she said for his ears only.

He agreed. This, he surmised, was not a home. It was bragging rights.

A short set of broad steps led to a grand porch—if you could call the architectural detail fronting a castle-like structure a porch.

The double doors opened as they approached. A woman, middle aged, well dressed, waited just inside.

"This way please." She gestured to the grand foyer.

Once they were across the threshold, the woman closed the doors, then led the way across the marble-floored foyer. The ceiling towered at least three stories, rising to the very top of the turret that fronted the mansion. They crossed under the upstairs landing that was flanked on either side by a stone staircase.

Jack had expected they would be ushered to a parlor of some sort, but instead the next set of double doors the woman opened revealed a library as large as the one in his hometown. The walls were lined with book-filled shelves. The flow was interrupted only by a large arched window on the opposite side from the doors, ensuring an inspiring view of the rear gardens. Near the window was a seating area, with a sofa and a couple of chairs surrounding a table.

A woman, her back turned, waited at the window that looked out over the meticulously and lushly cultivated landscape.

When the double doors closed, leaving Jack and Anne standing in the center of the room, the woman at the window turned to them. Eve Redford Langston took a couple of steps toward the seating area. Her attention first rested on Jack. It wasn't until she paused at the sofa that she shifted her attention to Anne. Her eyes widened. Jack was almost positive he heard a sharp intake of breath.

Eve gestured to the two upholstered chairs. "Sit. Please."

She lowered onto the sofa, her gaze tracking their movements toward the chairs.

When they were seated, she turned to Anne. "It's amazing how much you look like your mother."

IN THE PAST Anne would have stiffened if anyone had made such a remark to her, but somehow in the past few hours she had come to terms with many things. Her resemblance to her mother was one of them. It almost felt like a compliment.

"Thank you." She gazed steadily at the former best friend of Mary's. "And thank you for seeing us. Jack and I have a great deal of research to do."

The older woman's lips twitched in what might've been construed as a smile, but the effort was vague and lackluster.

"I assume the two of you are looking into your mother's history—at least, that's what I've heard. If that's the case, I'm happy to help any way I can."

Well, well. It seemed the kindly Judith had put the word out. Good. Anne had hoped she would. At the same time, Anne was a little disappointed.

The woman had claimed to be a friend of her mother's. Apparently that loyalty only went as far as the senator's address. Anne wondered if Jack had assumed or hoped for the same.

"We'd like to hear about the days and weeks leading up to the murder." Jack launched into the questions. "I've read the statements from the investigation, and they seem a tad incomplete."

"Incomplete?" Eve eyed him speculatively. "How so?"

"According to what we know, you, Mary Morton and Carin Carter Wallace spent a good deal of time together. You had been friends for many years at the time of the murder."

Eve made a single nod. "That's correct. You should have read as much in my statement."

"We did." Anne waded in. "My question is given the fact that you and Mary were so close, didn't you suspect or sense something was wrong—wrong enough to result in murder?"

The silence that followed echoed in the room like the nothingness that trailed a sonic blast.

Eve smiled then, something more than a mere twitch. She appeared to find the question amusing. "The detective asked me this as well."

"Your answer," Jack inserted, "was not documented in the file. There was some vague mention of you being out of town."

This time she actually laughed. The sound

was dry, half-hearted. "Detective Jones was young. Only a few years older than we were at the time. I'm not sure he had a clue what he was doing."

"Jack said the same thing," Anne pointed out. "It's insane that not a single appeal was granted considering the incompetent investigation and the subpar legal counsel Mary received."

Eve lifted her chin ever so slightly. "If that's how you feel, have you looked into what avenues you have to rectify those shortfalls? I can't imagine the city would want to enter into any sort of civil litigation. A settlement would likely be far more appealing."

Was the woman subtlety offering a payoff to shut Anne down? She didn't have to say the words outright. Anne saw it in her eyes—the anticipation. The offer was loud and clear. "So you agree there was negligence involved. Mary's conviction may have been a miscarriage of justice."

"Sadly, I don't agree." Eve sighed, crossed her hands on her lap. "As difficult as it was to believe in the beginning, I long ago faced the reality that Mary must have killed Neil. It was the only logical answer. Was the murder investigated as it should have been? Unquestionably not. Did she receive proper legal representation? Probably not. But that doesn't mean she wasn't guilty. If you're looking to clear her name, I must warn you that you will be gravely disappointed. You're far more likely to prove she wasn't properly represented by counsel."

Startled by the woman's certainty, Anne held up a hand. "I'm not looking to do anything but find the truth. That's why I need your help. You were her best friend, after all."

A standoff of sorts passed between them. Eve broke first.

"As your friend pointed out—" she gestured to Jack "—I was not here in the days that led up to the murder. Mary was busy with wedding plans and with her pregnancy. We didn't spend a lot of time together those final weeks."

"Where were you that final week before the murder?" Jack asked. "You stated that you were visiting your grandmother in Rockford, but I didn't find any statement from your grandmother confirming your alibi."

A hint of pink flushed her cheeks, and Anne barely resisted the urge to grin.

"It should be there," Eve argued. "Perhaps it was lost."

"Can anyone confirm you were at your grandmother's?" he asked.

"Well, since my grandmother is deceased, as are my parents," she admitted, "I suppose you'll have to take my word for it. She was ill at the time and needed me. My parents were on a month-long cruise."

"The prosecution suggested that Neil Reed was having an affair." Anne moved in a hopefully more constructive direction. "Were you aware of this? Did Mary give any indication of being worried about something like this?"

"She did mention having concerns about him." Eve's full attention turned to Anne. "Your mother was very intuitive. If Neil lied to her, she would have seen right through his efforts."

"If he was aware of this," Anne countered, "why would he bother lying? Then again, Mary had no history of violence. She didn't own a gun. There was never an explanation of where the gun came from."

"I'm afraid I have no idea. I can only say that she had concerns about her future husband. Perhaps it was merely cold feet." Eve lifted her hand toward Anne. "Or perhaps it was because she'd learned she was pregnant and any second thoughts were a little late. Whatever the case, she is the only person who could possibly have had a motive to kill Neil. There was no one else." She stood, obviously ready to dismiss them.

"One final question," Jack said as he, too, stood.

Anne followed suit. Hoped his question was

one that would leave the woman with something to think about.

Eve looked to him in expectation.

"Was Neil the one who introduced the senator to Michael Smith? It seems his work and investments in BioTech were very good moves." He glanced around the room. "Obviously it changed your life."

She blinked once, twice. "I'm afraid I have no idea. My husband served as lead counsel to Michael Smith and his company for a decade. I don't recall how they met. You would have to ask my husband, and he is very busy. He has to return to DC next week for the new session. I doubt he'll have time to meet with you before then."

"No problem," Jack insisted. "There are public records I can look through. I'm sure the senator disclosed his employment with and investment ties to BioTech when he took office."

"I'm sure." The senator's wife led the way back to the front door. She waited there and watched as they exited.

When she would have closed the door Anne decided to take one last shot at unsettling her. If the endgame was to rouse a reaction, they needed a good, strong final move.

"I've always wondered," she said to the woman standing in the doorway to her own private castle, "why no one—and you were her best friend—visited Mary in prison or helped with me after I was born. It was a shame I had to be thrust into foster care."

Eve stared at Anne for a long moment. "I can't speak for anyone else, but I can tell you that I was young and uncertain about my future. Kevin hadn't proposed, and frankly, I had no idea where my future was going. I simply couldn't take on the added responsibility." She looked away for a few seconds before meeting Anne's gaze once more. "It's a shame, though, what happened to you. I hope you won't allow the past to define your future."

When Anne and Jack were in his car driving away, she couldn't decide if she wanted to scream or to cry.

She had worked very hard not to allow her past to define her present or her future.

But this...this thing they were doing was different.

Wasn't it?

Suddenly she felt uncertain again. Why even go down this path? What did it matter, really?

"She wanted to make you feel unsure of yourself." Jack apparently read her mind.

"She did that rightly enough." Anne collapsed deeper into the seat and stared out the window. All those hurtful feelings related to her mother and the loneliness crushed in on her.

"I'm guessing," he said with a quick glance at her, "that we completely unhinged the lady. I'll bet she's on the phone right now calling her husband and demanding he take some sort of action."

A smile tugged at Anne's lips. "And next she'll call her friend Carin and warn her that the you-know-what is hitting the fan."

Jack laughed. "Exactly."

Anne drew in a really big breath and let it out slowly. "I swear it felt exactly like she was trying to tell me there was money to be had if I was willing to let this whole thing go."

"The conversation did take a bit of a turn in that direction. If that was her intent, she was definitely sly about it."

"Sly like a fox," Anne noted. "I'm getting this feeling that something is wrong where this BioTech business is concerned. Kevin Langston served as lead counsel for the start-up, but it sounded in the journal as if that was the position Neil was being considered for."

"I'll get someone looking into the possibility. Particularly now that we can make the connection between the friends."

"Thanks." Anne stared forward. "All right, so what's next?"

"I checked with the senior living community,

and we've been added to Mr. Reed's visitor's list."

"How did you manage that?" The fact that her pulse rate suddenly shot into rapid-fire had her feeling uncertain again. The man was her grandfather...and yet he had abandoned her just like everyone else.

"I can't give away all my secrets."

Anne laughed, the sound a little strangled. As long as his secret skills got the job done, she could live without knowing.

Reed Residence
The Sparkling Springs
Crystal Lake, 1:00 p.m.

THIS WAS DEFINITELY not your typical senior living community.

Anne surveyed the beautiful property as they walked from the parking area to the main office. The place was gated and, quite frankly, gorgeous. Nestled in a treed landscape, rows and rows of tiny cottages flanked the perimeter while taller apartment-style buildings filled the inner space. But everything between and around was like a park. Walking paths and ponds were bordered by lush shrubs and blooming plants. It was peaceful and elegant. It was amazing.

Not at all what Anne had expected.

They hadn't been able to come directly here after the meeting with Eve. Although Jack had called and provided all the necessary details required, Mr. Reed wasn't available for a visit until one. To kill time, they'd had lunch and discussed the senator's wife. They both agreed that she was nervous. Anne found Jack easy to talk to, and she continued to be surprised at how comfortable she felt with him and this deep dive into the past. She still had her moments of anxiety and trepidation, but not enough to make her hesitate.

"Does he have health issues?" she asked as they approached the grand entrance.

"Not that I've been able to determine. He has a huge real estate portfolio. The home where he lived with his family thirty years ago is sitting vacant now—much like the one Mary and Neil lived in—only well cared for. Last year, he suddenly moved here. If there was a health reason, he's kept it quiet."

Maybe all the memories had become too much for him.

Once in the main office lobby, they were met by a representative who signed them in, provided name badges and escorted them to Mr. Reed's door. He lived in one of the small cottages.

"Enjoy your visit," the representative said before scurrying away.

"Wow," Anne said quietly as they watched

her go. "This place is amazing. It must cost a small fortune."

Jack nodded. "Including all the fees, you're talking in the neighborhood of a hundred K per year."

Anne felt her eyes nearly pop out. Oh well, why not enjoy your later years being waited on hand and foot if you had the means?

Jack knocked on the door. "Hopefully the serene environment keeps him happy and cooperative."

Anne would appreciate cooperative.

The door opened, and an elderly man stared out at them. Despite his age, eighty, he stood tall and appeared strong and clear eyed. His hair was completely gray, and his attire looked as if he had an afternoon on the golf course planned—pressed khakis and a polo shirt.

He stared at Anne for a long moment before he spoke. "So you're the daughter."

In that instant it hit Anne fully, deeply that this man was her grandfather. An actual relative. She had no others. A man, she realized, who opted not to come for her after she was born in that prison infirmary. A man who allowed her to be thrust into foster care. A man who had abandoned her.

"And you're the grandfather," she said with perhaps more sarcasm than necessary.

He stared a moment more, then glanced at Jack. "Come in. Let's get this over with."

Now she was flat-out angry, but she did all in her power to keep the emotion to herself. Deep breaths and slow releases. She had Jack at her side. She could do this.

Once inside his cottage, she focused on the details around her rather than the man. The cottage was even lovelier inside than out. Nicely decorated and efficiently designed. Furnished for comfort but with an eye toward charm and sophistication.

"Join me." Preston Reed settled on the sofa.

He made no offer of refreshments, and that was just as well. Anne felt sick to her stomach. The shaking prompted by that blast of anger had started deep inside her and now spread through her limbs.

When they'd all taken seats, Jack said, "We appreciate your time, Mr. Reed."

Reed looked to Anne. "Why are you here?"

The man really knew how to get on her last nerve. "I—we—" she glanced at Jack "—are attempting to find answers about what really happened the day Neil was murdered."

Reed's expression remained passive, and he said nothing.

"The Colby Agency has looked into the way the investigation was conducted," Jack jumped in, drawing Reed's attention. "We don't believe the work was thorough. We'd like to remedy that."

The older man set his gaze on Anne once more. "The detective was young, probably not the best choice for the job. But I don't have any doubts as to the conclusion he reached. Mary killed my son. I'm certain of that."

"Why?" Anne held his gaze, her chin raised in defiance of his unwavering claim. "What makes you so certain?"

"Because my son said she would."

The words stunned Anne—hit her in the face like a blow from a closed fist.

"When did he say this?" Jack prodded. "Under what circumstances?"

"He'd decided to take a risk. He wanted to borrow against his trust fund and invest in some start-up company. She was against him taking a job with an up-and-coming company, so he thought an investment would be wise instead. He had come to see Mary's concerns about the risk considering she was unexpectedly pregnant."

Anne's breath caught softly before she could stop the reaction.

Reed scrutinized her for a moment before going on. "They wanted you. No need to worry about that. But you did show up before they'd planned to start a family."

She relaxed a little. "Why are you so convinced she would kill the father of her child?"

"Why do mothers kill their children?" He flung his arms upward. "Or fathers abandon their families? Who the hell knows? She wasn't crazy—I can tell you that. She was smart. Maybe a little too clever. All I know is she told Neil she would kill him, and that's what I told the police."

"When did she make this statement?" Anne pushed. He still hadn't explained that shocker to any real degree. And it sounded as if the statement was hearsay.

"He told me she said she would kill him if he dared take the risk of that position with a company just getting started." He stared at the floor a moment. "I don't think he really thought she would do it."

Anne glared at him, in part astonished but mostly just angry. "People say things like that all the time. It's just a way of getting the point across. It doesn't mean they really intend to kill the person to whom they made the statement."

"I felt that way too, until my son was dead."

Dear God. Anne barely resisted the need to roll her eyes. She already knew the answer to what she was about to ask, but it would be helpful to have it substantiated by someone who was there at the time. "What was the name of this company?"

He shook his head. "I don't recall. It's not relevant."

Anne wanted to shake him. He was purposely evading the question.

"We believe," Jack interjected, "Mary was innocent. We believe she was set up by someone close to her and Neil."

The silence that followed had Anne's heart starting to pound. If there was even a remote possibility the police had the wrong person, why had this man done nothing? If he'd felt the investigation wasn't thorough, why not hire a private detective? Why just sit back and let whatever would happen just happen? His son was dead! Murdered! Just because he believed his future daughter-in-law committed the crime did not make it true. For God's sake, he lost his son!

The mounting fury had her glaring at the man who was her grandfather. "Mary loved him. More than anything. She would not have killed him."

The journal... Anne fought to catch her breath. Even after all those years, Mary's love for Neil had been clear in her words.

Preston Reed looked away. "It doesn't matter. They're both dead now."

Fury slammed into her chest. "But I'm not and you're not. Why allow this travesty to stand?"

His gaze narrowed on her. "If it's money you want, you'll just have to wait for that. I've set up a trust fund that distributes to you when you reach age thirty. In, if memory serves, four months from now."

Anne drew back. "I didn't come here for your money." She launched to her feet. "I don't want your money. I want the truth."

Jack was at her side, a hand on her elbow. "We can go if you'd like," he offered.

Reed peered up at her, his face void of emotion. "Don't waste your time digging around in the past."

Anne couldn't speak. There were no words that accurately articulated what she wanted to say to him. Instead, she left. Couldn't get out of there fast enough.

Once they were in the car driving away, she said out loud, mostly to herself, "How could he ignore me all these years and then throw money at me?"

"It takes courage to step forward and do the right thing in times of loss. He was grieving the loss of his son—his only child. He may have seen you as an extension of Mary, and the idea of having you in his life was unbearable under the circumstances. But on some level, even now, he recognizes his obligation to his son's child."

She pressed her hands to her face, fought the urge to cry. Damn it. She would not cry. "When I agreed to do this, I didn't expect...this...*him*."

"There will be more." He glanced at her. "And some of it will be painful, maybe more than what just happened. But it's the only way to find what you're looking for."

Defeat crushed at her chest. He was right. But she had to be strong. She'd endured far more painful times growing up. On the scale of her childhood misery, this was nothing.

Chapter Nine

Crystal Lake
Farrell Residence
Bunker Lane, 3:00 p.m.

They stood outside the door of Beatrice Farrell's house. This was a cold call, so Jack wasn't sure how it would go.

Farrell was one of the teachers at Crystal Lake Elementary who had worked with Morton. She had been interviewed by the detective investigating the case, but she'd had no helpful information to share, according to his report.

She had retired at the end of this school year, so hopefully she was home and not traveling to celebrate her newfound freedom.

Anne pressed the doorbell a second time, and they continued to wait.

Jack had been a little worried about her after the visit with Preston Reed. She'd been more upset by the man than Jack had anticipated. He suspected all these years of ignoring the situation had not prevented Anne from forming feelings for the family she had never known except through newspaper clippings and online articles.

What little girl abandoned by a parent, whatever the circumstances, didn't dream of the fairy tale that could have been?

He hoped Farrell would be helpful. Of the three teachers who had been fairly close to Morton back then, Farrell was the only one still alive.

Finding someone who had relevant memories of Mary Morton and who was willing to share them would be good about now. Not only for the investigation but for Anne. She needed to see progress.

The door opened, and the woman who matched the photos from the school's website stood before them. Beatrice was petite, with hair that was more blond than gray and kept in a long braid. She had pale eyes, almost a blue, but they were actually a very light shade of silver. The knee-length shorts and cotton t-shirt she wore said she went for comfort over fashion. Judging by her weathered skin and the sheer number of blooming plants in her landscape, she liked spending her free time outside.

She looked to Jack. "I'm sure you noticed the no-soliciting sign next to the sidewalk."

"Mrs. Farrell," Anne said, drawing her attention, "my name is Anne Griffin."

Farrell shifted her attention toward Anne. Her hand went to her mouth. "Oh my word, you're Mary's daughter."

Jack watched Anne's reaction. This just kept happening. If she'd had any doubts about how much she looked like her mother, she shouldn't have any now. He'd noticed the remarkable resemblance the first time he googled her.

Anne produced a realistic smile. "I am."

Maybe she was getting attached—or at least accustomed—to the idea.

The older woman pressed her hand to her chest now. "I was so sorry to hear that she passed." She smiled sadly. "I wrote to her every month all these years." She shrugged. "Even though she never wrote me back, I felt it was the least I could do considering everyone else had turned on her."

The relief on Anne's face was palpable. "Would you have a few minutes for us to ask some questions about Mary and the time surrounding...what happened?"

"Of course." Farrell drew the door open wider. "Come in."

Jack followed Anne, then closed the door since Farrell was busy explaining how her husband had passed away last year and now it was just her.

He followed the two to the kitchen, where Farrell insisted on putting on a pot of tea. The house was a typical ranch style. A good-sized yard surrounded it, all enclosed with an aged picket fence. A gray cat appeared, rubbed against its master's legs and then eyed Jack suspiciously before disappearing.

"Sit at the table with me." Farrell ushered them to the dining table.

The kitchen-dining combo was just off the living room. You could actually see both the front and back doors from the table.

"I have lots of questions for you," Farrell said to Anne, "but you go first. I'm sure yours are far more important than mine."

"Thank you." Anne accepted a cup of tea from their host.

"Would you like cream or sugar?" Farrell asked.

"No, thank you." Anne cradled the fragile cup in both hands as if she needed the warmth.

Farrell looked to Jack. "The same for me."

When the lady had poured a cup for Jack and then one for herself, she turned back to Anne. "Please, ask away."

"First," she began, "you said you wrote to Mary. But she never once wrote you back?"

Farrell shook her head. "No, she didn't, but I understood. The lack of a response never put me off. I continued to write to her. Usually only a page, but something to let her know I was thinking of her."

"That was very kind of you. Before the murder, were you aware of any issues between Mary and Neil?"

Farrell shook her head. "Absolutely not. Those two were madly in love. The only time I ever heard her mention being upset with Neil was when he wanted to accept that position with some start-up company." She frowned, set her cup aside as if holding it splintered her concentration. "They'd just found out about you." She smiled at Anne. "Mary was worried that some start-up company wouldn't provide the stability they would need going forward with a baby on the way."

"Do you remember the name of the company?" Jack asked. There was mention of Neil's offer from a start-up company, but the journal never mentioned the name.

Farrell appeared to ponder the question for a time. "I can't... Wait. Bio something, I think. Some sort of medical something." She shook her head. "Sorry. I swear the memory is the first thing to go once you pass sixty."

"I feel that way," Anne said, "and I'm not even thirty."

"Life is busy," Farrell said. "Too much on our minds these days."

"Some have suggested," Anne went on, "that Neil was cheating on Mary."

Another firm shake of her head. "Absolutely not. I would have known." She laughed softly. "I wasn't Mary's closest friend, but we teachers spend so much time together discussing students and the headaches and heartaches of being an educator that we're bound to share personal difficulties. She would have told me. I'm certain. She adored Neil and never spoke negatively of him. Never."

"Do you," Jack said, "remember anything at all that gave you pause during the days that led up to the murder?"

Farrell took a moment before she answered. "The only thing I recall is that Mary was furious with her friend Eve—you know, the senator's wife." She cringed an unpleasant expression. "It was the first time I'd heard Mary sound so put out by her. I think they were friends since childhood."

"Did she mention any specific trouble?"

Farrell hesitated for five or so seconds but then looked at Anne. "I swore to Mary that I would never tell this." She sighed. "I suppose it doesn't matter now that she's gone." Farrell tilted her head and frowned. "Not that I would tell a soul except you."

She inhaled a big breath as if what she had to

say was quite the burden. "Mary was looking into how to do a reliable paternity test without Neil knowing anything about it. She couldn't let him find out."

Anne drew back as if the woman had slugged her. "What?"

"I'm so sorry. If Mary didn't tell you this, then I'm guessing she found a way and determined that all was as it should be." She stared into her cup a moment. "I probably shouldn't have told you." Her gaze lifted to Anne's once more. "But Mary was beside herself about it for reasons she never explained. Of course, it was easy enough to assume the reason. I suppose Eve didn't agree with some aspect of the situation. Whatever the case, the two were out of sorts."

Jack watched Anne carefully to ensure she was going to hold it together after that revelation. There certainly hadn't been anything in the diary about another love interest.

Anne moistened her lips. "You're right. I didn't know, but now it's important that I know everything possible if I'm going to find the truth."

"Do you know if she spoke to Eve or to her other friend, Carin about this?" Jack chimed in, hoping to usher things forward. He felt bad at the sorrow clouding Anne's eyes.

"I don't know." Farrell picked up her tea once more. "I actually found out by accident. It was

Mary's planning period, and her class was in the gym. It was mine as well. My class was in art, but I went to the gym for a personal reason. The PE instructor at the time was my husband's first cousin. We were planning a cookout that weekend, so I popped into the gym to run the date and time by him."

"Was Mary in the gym?" Anne asked.

"No. No. She was in her classroom." A frown furrowed across the older woman's brow. "As I walked into the gym one of Mary's third graders stopped playing and started crying. She said she didn't feel well and wanted to go home." Her gaze grew distant as if the memory was playing like a movie reel in her mind. "Suddenly the little girl fell to the floor and had a seizure. While Winston, our cousin, saw to her, I ran to the nurse's office. I sent her to the gym, then I rushed to Mary and told her what had happened. She hurried out of the room, and I collapsed into her chair to catch my breath."

"Was the little girl okay?"

Farrell nodded at Anne. "Oh, yes. A fever caused the seizure. She had a thorough checkup and spent a few days at home, and then she was fine."

Farrell hesitated a moment. "When I stood to go from Mary's room I noticed a brochure open on her desk. I didn't mean to be nosy, but it was right there. Later, I asked her if everything was all right, and she broke down into tears and said she had to be sure about who the father was before she and Neil could move ahead with their wedding plans."

Her face pale, Anne tackled the next realistic question. "Was she planning an abortion if things didn't turn out the way she hoped?"

The hollow sound of her voice tore at Jack.

"Oh, no," Farrell insisted. "She'd already picked out names and nursery furniture. She said she just had to know so she could tell Neil. She was adamant that he should know the truth."

When Anne said nothing more, Jack asked, "Mrs. Farrell, did Mary mention who the father might be if not Neil Reed?"

Another fervent shake of her head. "No. She wouldn't talk about it. When I asked she grew very upset…angry, even." She looked Jack directly in the eyes. "But I can tell you one thing for certain—Mary Morton was a good woman. Kind and loyal to a fault. Whatever happened, she didn't mean for it to happen. As good a person as she was, she was only human." Beatrice shook her head again. "Still, I cannot imagine how the situation came about. The next thing I knew, Neil was dead and Mary had been charged with his murder. I tried to see her, but they wouldn't let me. They said she didn't want to see me, but I didn't believe them."

"Did you tell the police about the paternity test?"

Farrell looked away. When she turned back to Anne, tears sat on her lashes. "No, I didn't. Because I believed with all my heart that Mary would never have hurt Neil or anyone else. I wasn't about to give them any more ammunition to use against her."

"I'm sure she appreciated that," Anne said softly. "Do you recall the name of the lab?"

"Well, you would think so. I stared at the brochure for several seconds. I guess I was a bit stunned. But I don't recall the name. It's been a long time."

Anne nodded.

When the silence lingered, Jack pulled a business card from his pocket and passed it to the former teacher. "I hope you'll call if you think of anything at all that might help us."

She stared at the card a moment and nodded, then she placed it on the table. Her hand went to Anne's. "I am so sorry if this news hurt you, but please don't hold it against your mother. However the question of paternity came about, she suffered enough when Neil was murdered."

"I guess I don't understand. If Mary was such a good person, why did no one stand up for her at trial?" Anne held up a hand. "I recognize that you did by not telling the police about the paternity test, but why no one else? No other teacher? None of her other friends? No one?"

The pain in her voice and on her face twisted a knot in Jack's gut. He had known this would be hard. But that didn't make watching it happen any easier.

"Perhaps you don't realize how powerful Preston Reed was at the time," Beatrice said quietly. "Throughout his life he has stayed behind the scenes. Never put himself out there for political office. But make no mistake—he ran things. Three days after his son was murdered, his wife had a heart attack and died. He was devastated. The rumor was that he blamed Mary for his wife's death as well as his son's. No one would have dared to step on Preston's toes. Your mother was doomed from the moment she was charged."

Anne thanked Mrs. Farrell, but she didn't say another word until they were in the car driving away.

"Is there a way to find out what lab she used?" She turned to face Jack.

"We can try." He slowed for the upcoming turn. "The one she used may have gone out of business or been gobbled up by another one, so I wouldn't count on finding the exact place."

Anne sat back in her seat and chewed on her lips. "She mentioned in the journal about an issue, but she also said that it turned out okay." She shook her head. "That was also the point when she mentioned her friends had basically abandoned her. It has to mean something. The trouble—the new job—all of it was somehow connected."

"I agree, and my money is on Langston. After all, he was one of the best friends. The chances of an encounter occurring were far more likely and would certainly have created the rift between Mary and Eve."

"Could have been another teacher," Anne argued. "Or the principal."

Jack shrugged. "Could have been. But schools aren't exactly the best place for secrets. I would bet money that someone—Mrs. Farrell, for sure—would have known if something was going on there." He sent Anne a sideways look. "I don't know about you, but I got the impression Mrs. Farrell felt the incident would not have been something Mary agreed to."

Anne stared out her window. "Maybe she just doesn't want to think badly of Mary."

Jack wasn't going any further down that road. Although, next to money, an affair was a major motive discovered in murder investigations. The biggest sticking point in Jack's opinion was the fact that her closest friends, meaning the Langstons and Carin Carter Wallace, hadn't appeared to know. Based on the statements the three gave in court, if they had known anything else negative, it would have come out of their mouths.

Unless...it involved the future senator.

Jack's attention shifted to the rearview mirror. A black sedan had been following them since leaving Farrell's neighborhood.

Coincidence? Maybe.

Only one way to find out.

"Brace yourself." Jack made a sudden right.

The tires squealed. Anne grabbed the armrest, then shot him a look. "What the heck, Jack?"

The sedan didn't make the turn.

Jack relaxed the narrowest margin. "Almost missed my turn." He didn't want to worry her until he had no choice.

"Maybe next time you could give me a little more warning."

"You got it." But then, at the next intersection, he swore under his breath.

The black sedan had taken a right at the next block. It was back.

The driver was male. Sunglasses on.

"Brace yourself again." Jack punched the accelerator and made a hard left.

He continued to turn here and there until he was confident the sedan wasn't reappearing.

When he felt it was safe to slow down, he glanced at his passenger. "You up for an early dinner?"

She sent him a pointed look, her grip on the dash loosening. "If it means you'll stop driving like a crazy person."

He laughed. The sedan by now would be waiting for them at their hotel since he wasn't able to keep up. "Sorry about that, but we had a tail, and I wanted to give him a hard time."

She groaned. "They're already watching us?"

"They are. Actually, I'm surprised it took this long." He flashed her a smile. "But this is good."

Anne made a face. "If you say so."

"It means they're worried," he explained. "If they had nothing to hide they wouldn't be worried."

She turned to him, and a smile spread across her pretty face. "You're right. This is good."

Chapter Ten

Journal Entry
Thirty Years Ago
July 15

I realized by then that I had no true friends. There were my colleagues at work who were nice and whom I adored working with, but we were not friends in the true sense of the word. I was getting a little paranoid actually. At least the other worry had passed. The lab results were what I had hoped for. But I won't talk about that since it worked out for the best. Thank God. I don't think I could have lived with myself if it had turned out differently.

Still, Neil was considering a new venture for after he graduated next year. It was a start-up company that he felt would explode with opportunity in the near future. He was offered a part-time position starting late July. The trouble was that the company was untried. He would be brand new out of law school and serving as the company's head legal counsel. It was quite the prestigious offer for him, except for all the reasons I just named.

By then you would have been born and maybe even trying to crawl. But I didn't want to go back to work that first year. I really wanted to spend some time being your mom. The health insurance was the issue. At the time, my insurance was with my work. Who knew what this new company just starting out would offer. If I took a year off, there might not have been any health insurance. That would not have worked. I told myself that Neil would make the right decision.

Carin had not come back, and by this point Eve and I were not speaking. It was awful the way we had fallen apart. All for such stupid reasons…all because of one person.

By that point I realized I should have told Neil the truth when it happened, and this would have been behind us. But I didn't, and by mid-July I was living with that nightmare hanging over my head. I had no idea what the right thing to do was. I was so young. Neil's life was so busy with his last year of law school and the decisions about our future. He had no time for distraction.

The best I could do was hope all would work out and we could move forward with our lives and never look back. Even then I had begun to believe we had outgrown our friends anyway.

It was time to make new friends. I didn't want to raise a child with friends like our old ones.

With that in mind, I told myself we would get through it and maybe in a couple of years we would try for another child. It would have been so wonderful to have a boy and a girl. I remember thinking these things. Although I hadn't had a scan yet, I was convinced you would be a girl. If that turned out to be the case, I planned to name you Marianne. The *Mari* part after me, of course, and the *Anne* after Neil's mom. She was such a good mom and wife. Far better than her husband deserved. I hoped I could be half as good as she was. Just so you know, it wasn't because my mother was a bad one. She just wasn't the kind of mom I wanted to be. I loved her, but I wanted to be better.

I often sat in our little cottage and wondered if one day we would have a bigger house. I even pondered the idea that I should be thankful Neil was considering that start-up company. If it went the way he believed it would, we could end up very comfortable. Possibly even rich.

Maybe some things were worth the risk.

I had decided to talk to him about it again. Just because we were having a baby we shouldn't have been afraid to go for a better life.

I was happy with the decision, and I couldn't wait to tell Neil.

But I had no idea what was coming.

Chapter Eleven

Crystal Lake
Friday, July 11
Latham & Hirsh Law Firm
Virginia Street, 10:00 a.m.

Anne was on edge this morning. She had been since she awakened at five o'clock. Walking the floors of her room for an hour hadn't helped. Then finally around six or so she'd gone outside and stared at the water in hopes the serenity of its stillness would help her find her center.

Hadn't happened.

By seven she'd gone back inside and made a cup of coffee. She couldn't stop thinking about the house where Mary and Neil had lived or the details Beatrice Farrell had shared with her. Specifically, the idea that Neil might not be the father of the child Mary had been carrying.

Her father, Anne amended. She was trying—she really was—to get right with consistently acknowledging the people who had brought her into this world. Not so easy after all these years of resentment and of pretending they didn't exist or were irrelevant. Growing up, she had learned to turn off those feelings. It was the only way to protect herself.

She pushed aside the thought. That little girl no longer needed protecting. She was a grown woman, and she owed it to herself—and maybe to her parents—to do this. The journal had mentioned some sort of situation Mary had worried about and that it had been straightened out. Anne had no idea what the problem—or situation—was until yesterday. Obviously it was the concern about paternity.

When Jack knocked on the door to her room this morning and let her know it was time to go, she'd been startled. She had been far too deep in the swarm of new discoveries to notice the passage of time. After the murder, her mother had basically gone through the horrors of her situation alone. Her own parents were long dead. Her friends had abandoned her. She really was completely alone.

For the first time in her entire life, Anne felt sympathy for the woman who had given birth to her. Perhaps those feelings were misguided. After all, being here and talking to the people who had known Mary and Neil made all of it so real. Quite honestly the whole story—what little she had known about it—had seemed like a work of fiction to Anne. Not part of her actual life. Nothing she had actually experienced.

As a child she'd experienced only resentment and disappointment related to her biological parents. But this had changed everything far faster than she could have imagined possible. Had Victoria, the head of the Colby Agency, known this would happen? Was that why she insisted Anne participate in the investigation?

Anne would hold off until this was done before thanking her…or not.

Too many confusing emotions roiled inside her just now to visualize how this would all settle down.

Since today was forecast to be another scorcher, she had selected her lightest-weight blouse and the blue dress pants. It was important to represent herself well at this meeting, given that she was also representing her parents, so to speak.

It really was the oddest, somewhat unsettling urge.

"You ready?"

Jack's voice dragged her attention back to the present for the second time this morning. They were here—at the office where Neil had worked part-time during his final year of law school and the final months and weeks of his life. Anne blinked. She hadn't realized they had arrived or that the car had stopped. She gave herself a mental shake. Keeping her focus on the now was far too important to be allowing herself to get caught up in the what-ifs and oh-my-gods of thirty years ago.

Jack looked from her to the office building in front of them. He had taken the last parking slot on the same side of the street. Mr. Hirsh would see them at 10:15. He was the only remaining partner who had been with the firm for more than thirty years—making him the only one who had known Neil Reed. Without hesitation, he had agreed to the meeting. No questions. But that had been late yesterday. Maybe sleeping on the idea will have changed his mind. He might share nothing at all or have questions of his own. Anne wouldn't be surprised either way.

"Anne?"

She jerked to attention once more. "Yes. Sorry. I'm ready." Anne reached for the door.

Jack did the same. They met on the sidewalk at the front of the car. He'd finally learned not to bother rushing to her side of the vehicle to open the door. It was so not necessary, and she felt foolish waiting for him to do so. Still, the notion that he would if she opted to go that route was refreshing in an old-fashioned sort of way. There was something to be said for chivalry. She was pretty much convinced that he was a very nice man.

Despite her determination there was no stopping him from opening the door to the law firm for her. She thanked him with a smile and walked in. At the reception desk, she deferred to Jack. He had made the call for the meeting.

"Good morning," Sandra, according to the nameplate, announced.

"Good morning. Jack Brenner and Anne Griffin to see Mr. Hirsh."

After checking the calendar, Sandra nodded. "He's ready for you now." She stood. "This way, please."

They followed her along a carpeted corridor. Paintings of the partners, retired or deceased ones first, lined the walls. At the end of the corridor was a table topped with a large, lush flower arrangement. Reminded Anne a little of a funeral home.

Sandra rapped on the door to the left, then opened it. "Mr. Hirsh, your ten fifteen is here." She swept her right hand in a gesture for Anne and Jack to enter the office.

The gray-haired gentleman behind the gleaming, wide wooden desk stood. "Thank you, Sandra."

She left the room, closing the door behind her.

"Mr. Brenner, I presume," Hirsh said to Jack before turning to Anne. "Ms. Griffin. Take a seat, and let's dive in. I worked you in between appointments, so my time is limited."

"Thank you for that," Jack said as he waited for Anne to settle. Then he claimed the chair next to her.

Always the gentleman, she mused.

"As I told your assistant, I'm from the Colby Agency—a private investigations firm in Chicago," Jack explained, cutting straight to the chase. "We have questions about Neil Reed."

Mr. Hirsh clasped his hands on his desk. "Well, that goes back a bit. Neil interned here for a few months as I'm sure you're aware. We had high hopes for him. He was a brilliant student of the law. The goal was when he graduated and passed the bar to work with Oscar Nelson. Oscar was nearing retirement age, and we wanted to get someone good on board to absorb as much of his wisdom as possible before that happened. We felt Neil was a promising young man with a natural gift for the work we do here."

"When was the decision made that he would join your firm?" Jack inquired. "We've found some indication that he had other plans."

"BioTech." Hirsh nodded. "I believe that was his first choice, but there was a glitch, as I recall, and he opted to take the offer we made."

"Glitch?" Anne echoed, speaking for the first time.

The attorney's attention shifted to her. "I can't say for certain, of course, since those details were never made public or shared with anyone at this firm. The rumor was that Mike Smith, the BioTech CEO, withdrew the offer and hired someone else."

They knew part of this already. Jack's research department at the Colby Agency determined that Langston had taken the position instead of her father. But no one appeared to know how that change came about. And as Hirsh said, any fallout was kept under wraps. The whole ordeal took place so quietly and so far behind the scenes it was as if it never happened...except it had, and Anne's instincts warned it had served as an impetus for the storm that descended on Mary Morton's and Neil Reed's lives.

Frankly, to Anne's way of thinking, anything kept so secretive couldn't have been good for all parties involved.

"We've learned that Neil and his fiancée," Anne said, "were concerned about BioTech being new without the potential security and benefits of a more established firm like yours. Perhaps that was the only glitch."

"I'd like to think," Hirsh said, "that our package was the better offer, and that was the reason we were able to lock him in well in advance of his being able to join us as an attorney. But there was talk to the contrary."

Anne was surprised he opted to share what was clearly hearsay.

"Did you or any of the partners," Jack probed, "at the time have any concerns or hesitations before making the offer? He was months from graduating, and then there was the bar exam after that. How could you be certain he'd pull it all off?"

"One only needed to review his transcript to know that—barring a grave illness or death—there was no question Neil Reed would do those things and do them particularly well. The fact is if you expect to get the best coming out of law school, you have to make the preliminary offers early. We learned that lesson the hard way. It's a situation that continues to be a concern with maintaining a larger firm, which is why we've downsized somewhat in recent years."

"In the days before his murder," Anne ventured, "were you aware of any issues going on in his private life? Did he seem worried or upset here at the office?"

"We've read the statement you made to the investigating detective," Jack pointed out. "What we're in search of is anything that, looking back, may have been more important than you realized at the time."

A very good point, in Anne's opinion, since Hirsh's statement told them basically nothing other than Neil was brilliant, dependable and charming.

"In particular," Anne tossed in while Hirsch pondered Jack's question, "any issues between Neil and Kevin Langston? Perhaps there was bad blood after the way things turned out with the BioTech offer." The fact that Hirsh hadn't mentioned Langston in connection to the so-called glitch was certainly no indication that he didn't know. She would wager that he was well aware.

The hesitation dragged on a bit. Jack pulled out his phone and checked it as if to show his impatience. Anne, on the other hand, kept her attention fixed on the attorney. She wanted that answer. There had to be an issue between the two men. Everything pointed in that direction.

"It was my opinion," Hirsh said finally, "that there was a rift between the two men afterward, yes."

"Can you elaborate on that?" Jack tucked his phone away.

"Not really. Whatever issues arose from the quandary, I'm sure the two worked those out. But, of course, I have no way of knowing those private details. Frankly it takes little or no imagination to recognize it was an issue. Neil never spoke of it or of his friend which, in my opinion, was telling in itself."

"That would suggest the two didn't work out

the issues at all," Anne tossed in. "Neil was murdered soon after. If there was some underhanded step that caused Langston to steal the position Neil had already accepted, that's the sort of story that makes life complicated for a politician."

Anne understood before she made the statement that Hirsh would have no comment, but she wanted him to realize she wasn't blind. What Langston did was motive whether he killed Neil or not. The bigger question was why the police didn't investigate that avenue.

Hirsh's expression closed instantly. "I'm afraid I am unaware of any such step. Senator Langston has a long-standing reputation of exceptional accomplishments in this city and in representing this state. I would be remiss if I didn't warn you that such unfounded rumors can be constituted as libelous. Which is why I shall refrain from further comment."

"This is exactly the sort of brick wall," Jack remarked, "as I'm sure you're aware, that prevents those searching from finding the truth."

"Well." Hirsh stood. "I hope I've been of some assistance to you. I do have another appointment waiting. Good luck with your endeavor."

Anne and Jack had almost made it to the door when he hesitated and turned back to the attorney. "Just one other thing. Did your firm handle the nondisclosure agreement for the senator when a former intern came forward accusing him of sexual assault?"

Anne stared at Jack for a moment, shock radiating through her. This was certainly news to her. She quickly banished the reaction and turned to Hirsh to hear the answer. Inside, she couldn't stop wondering why Jack hadn't mentioned a sexual-assault accusation in Langton's history. She certainly hadn't found anything even remotely negative related to the man in her searches. His history—according to the World Wide Web—was as clean as a whistle.

Hirsh's face blanched. "As I'm sure *you* are aware, I can't discuss the work we do at this firm unless, of course, you are in need of one or more of those services."

Jack smiled. "Never mind. I have the answer now."

They exited the office. Anne barely kept her mouth shut until they were outside and in the car. "You didn't mention anything about a sexual-assault accusation."

"I just found out—that text I received a few minutes ago."

"You have someone still digging?" The frustration drained away, and she had to admit she was impressed.

He shifted in his seat, faced her. "To be clear,

our people will be working on finding whatever there is to find until this is done."

"Okay." Talk about the full treatment. She couldn't ask for more than that. She also couldn't stop looking into his eyes. He really did have nice eyes, but it was the certainty, the reassurance there that had her lingering.

He turned back to the steering wheel, reversed out of the slot and headed for Williams Street. They were having an early lunch at Judith's. Jack wanted to rattle her cage again. Anne was fully on board with the plan.

As he drove in that direction, she chewed at her lip. "I'm thinking that if your discovery is illustrative of the sort of man Langston is or was, he could very well have forced an encounter with Mary. That may be why she wanted the paternity test. It makes the most sense—don't you think?"

Something definitely happened between the longtime friends. Maybe it was money, aka the BioTech position, *and* sex. Maybe one or the other, but it had happened. All they had to do was prove it.

"I think it's a strong possibility."

Or maybe Anne only wanted it to be Langston after the things she had learned he'd done. Stealing the job Neil had hoped for. Abusing an intern. On the other hand, in both instances, they were hearing just one side of the story. Maybe more so than ever, she recognized that there were two sides to every story.

She wished it hadn't taken her so long to realize this. Perhaps she should have tried visiting her mother again. Maybe if she hadn't stopped Mary would have eventually given in before it was too late. Anne would never know about that. All she could do was keep digging until someone told the truth.

What they needed was to talk to the senator. Anne considered herself pretty good at spotting untruths and insincerities. She'd certainly felt seriously bad vibes from Eve Langston. They also very much needed to get an interview with Carin Carter Wallace. She was closer to the Langstons than anyone else. Anne imagined the woman was privy to all their secrets.

Jack pulled out his cell phone and accepted a call.

While he spoke quietly with the caller, Anne pondered the well-prepared answers they had gotten from Hirsh. The man had wanted to appear cooperative with his little well-couched innuendos. She had a feeling the only thing he had done was give answers that would lead absolutely nowhere. And if his firm had represented Langston before…perhaps they still did. In which case, his agreement to meet with them was in all likelihood just an opportunity to get information for the senator.

If Jack had the name of the woman who'd claimed the assault—

"We have to go back to the hotel," Jack announced before she'd finished the thought.

"Why? Did you forget something?"

His hands tightened on the steering wheel. "There was a fire in your room. Several rooms along that corridor suffered smoke damage." He glanced at her. "We'll need to find a new place to stay."

He'd lost her at *a fire in your room.* "How in the world did that happen?" The possibilities swirled in her head. She had not used an iron or a hair dryer or any other product that required electricity except the coffeemaker which stayed plugged in. She hadn't touched it other than to brew a cup of coffee. Whatever happened, she didn't think it was related to her use of the room.

"At the moment they don't know the cause. Only that it started in your room."

In her opinion that said it all. Anne sank into the seat. Did someone want them to stop their investigation that badly? Desperately enough to do this?

Thank God she had the box and all its contents with her.

What about the photos? She grabbed her purse

and dug through it. A deep breath was impossible until her fingers found those irreplaceable photos. They were there. Thank God.

If she'd left them in the room...

She shook off the thought. She hadn't.

The secrets and the lies and now a fire? It had been almost thirty years since Neil Reed was murdered and Mary Morton went to prison. What could anyone be trying to hide at this point?

Fear slid cold and oily through her chest.

There was only one answer—the truth about who murdered Neil Reed.

Just like Mary Morton said.

Water's Edge Hotel
Chapel Hill Road, Johnsburg, Noon

JACK STARED AT the blackened walls, the burned bed and curtains, the partially melted and charred desk and chair that had been a part of Anne's room. He was damned glad they had already left before this thing started. But then, whoever did this had known they weren't in their rooms. The goal was to destroy any evidence Anne might have left in the room and to scare her.

If Jack had doubted the conclusion, the fire marshal confirmed it by admitting that arson was suspected.

"Did anything survive?" Anne asked when he walked to where she waited near the stairwell at the end of the corridor.

"I wouldn't think so. Either way, they aren't going to give us access to the room or its contents anytime soon."

"We'll need new rooms." She sighed. "And clothes."

"Agreed." He glanced around. "We can do that now if you're ready."

She looked up at him. "I say we go to Judith's as planned. While we wait for the food, I'll look for a new hotel online, and you check in with the senator's people again. I want to see that man today."

Jack couldn't help but grin. She'd been so hesitant about going along with this investigation, and now she was leading the charge. He loved it.

She frowned. "Why are you smiling?"

"Just thinking how lucky I am to have you as a partner on this. What a good plan." He hitched his head toward the parking lot. "You ready? If the manager here needs anything else he has my number."

As they walked away she grumbled something about *partner* and shot him a look, but the smile her expression melted into told him she kind of liked the idea. He did too. Maybe too much.

When they reached the car, Jack held up a

hand. "Hang on." With the fire in the rooms, he wasn't taking any risks that whoever had started it might not decide on some other route to deter them.

He checked the car doors—still locked. No way anyone was opening the hood or the trunk without getting into the car. Then he got down onto his hands and knees on the pavement, lowered onto his back and had a look at the undercarriage. He checked all the way around the vehicle and in the wheel wells.

No tracking devices. No other unexpected additions. He got to his feet and dusted himself off.

"You think they would try to tamper with the car?" Fear made its way into her eyes.

"At this point, we can't pretend it isn't a possibility."

She dusted off the back of his shirt, stopping at his waist. "The idea is a little unsettling, but I suppose I shouldn't be surprised."

"It is unsettling." He rested his gaze on hers then. "Being extra careful is the guide now. We don't do anything without being abundantly cautious."

"Got it." She made a face. "You see this kind of thing in the movies. On the news. You just don't expect to have it happen in your real life."

"I can talk to Victoria." Worry nudged him. "Maybe I should finish this on my own."

"No way." She shook her head firmly from side to side. "I'm all in—especially now. I'm not going anywhere until this is done. I'm your partner, you said," she reminded him.

"All right, then. But if you change your mind at any point, say the word."

He had a feeling that would never happen. This lady was tougher than she looked.

Just another thing he liked about her. Truth was he liked everything about her.

Chapter Twelve

Barrington
Langston Residence
Plum Tree Road, 3:00 p.m.

Anne could barely remain seated. They had arrived and were shown to the senator's home office. The room was exactly what she had expected. Lots of dark wood, a massive desk and a wall filled with shelves in the same dark walnut. Each shelf was lined with law books. If he arrived wearing a tweed jacket and smoking a pipe her visual image would be complete.

Though the design was quite traditional, it felt heavy and outdated. The space needed a serious update, in Anne's opinion.

Jack glanced at her. She managed a smile. He would be wondering if she was anxious. The answer was yes. She was nervous for sure. But learning all possible from and about this man was essential. She would do whatever was necessary to make that happen.

Except she really didn't want to die trying to find answers.

The memory of how the aftermath in her hotel room had looked and smelled haunted her. If she sniffed her blouse the odor still lingered. The fire marshal had mentioned that the fire had moved fast. They would be testing for an accelerant, which he suspected would be found. Whoever set that fire hadn't been playing around. Sadly, the hotel had no security cameras, and no one they had questioned so far had seen a single thing out of the ordinary.

Deep inside, she shivered at the thought of how someone could have been injured or killed because she had kicked a hornet's nest. It was impossible to ignore the fact that someone or several someones did not want the truth dug up and were willing to do anything to stop it.

Was finding a thirty-year-old truth really worth the risk to her safety and that of others?

Then again, if she didn't finish this, it could happen again. If the senator was the one who murdered Neil, then he could still be hurting people. Case in point, the sexual-assault allegation. She could only imagine what he might be capable of in the future. He certainly had no place in a position of such significant power.

If he was the one, he had to be stopped.

The door opened and the man himself walked

in. She and Jack stood. Part of her had wanted to stay seated. He wasn't royalty, just another possibly crooked politician. Maybe a killer... certainly an abuser. She suddenly felt foolish for showing him any regard whatsoever.

"I apologize for keeping you waiting." He paused and thrust out his hand, first to Anne.

She brushed her palm against his, barely touching his hand. "Anne Griffin."

Jack took his hand next, gave it a firm pump. "Jack Brenner."

The senator was a tall man. Even nearing sixty, the only gray in his hair was at his temples. He carried himself with an air of importance—as if anyone he encountered should recognize his worth. There were many things Anne instantly recognized about the man—arrogant, self-serving, to name a few. But then, she'd drawn that conclusion before he set foot in the room.

He skirted his desk and settled into the leather chair behind it. "I understand you're conducting some sort of investigation into Neil Reed's murder." His attention moved between the two of them coming to rest on Jack. "I'm familiar with the Colby Agency's stellar reputation. I'm sure you'll be thorough."

"We appreciate your time, Senator. Our primary goal at this time is to determine what was happening in Mary Morton's and Neil Reed's personal lives just before the murder. We've reviewed the official case file and, frankly, found it lacking. Perhaps it was inexperience on the detective's part. Given the many holes in the work, we're basically going over all the steps."

Langston leaned back in his chair, his forearms and hands resting on the chair arms. "My wife mentioned that you spoke with her already." He glanced at Anne for the first time since they brushed palms. "Eve was right. You do look so much like your mother."

Anne forced a smile. "You and your wife were very close to my parents. Were you aware of any trouble between them or with any of their friends just before the murder?" Like *you*, she wanted to say but did not. Who could doubt the possibility considering what this man had taken from Neil Reed? Even if he wasn't guilty of murder, he knew things—things that could make a difference.

He paused for consideration of the question before responding. "I was unaware of any personal trouble between Mary and Neil. As for issues with friends, I can't say that the relationship he and I once had was the same. Obviously not, since I was chosen over him for a position he really wanted. But like politics, the field of law is competitive. Fiercely so. There are no in-betweens. You're either winning or you're losing. In that case, I was the winner."

Anne bit her lips together to hold back the retort that sprang to the tip of her tongue.

"What about your relationship with Mary?" Jack said. "Was their trouble between you and Reed where she was concerned?"

Like the attorney they had met with this morning, Langston's face cleared of emotion. He turned his hands up as if to say he didn't understand the question. But then he spoke. "Mary and Eve were very good friends. Best friends, I would say," he insisted. "I, of course, was friends with her as well but only through Eve. There was never anything beyond that between Mary and me. She was busy with her teaching, and I was even busier with building my career. We hardly had time for anything else. I can't imagine where you stumbled upon such an idea."

Stumbled? Anne bit her teeth together hard to prevent a retort.

Jack looked from Anne to Langston, she suspected to build the anticipation of his next question. "Was there anyone else," he pressed, "close to the four of you who may have taken an unsolicited interest in Mary?"

"Are you implying Mary had an affair?" Langston's tone was imbued with surprise or something on that order. Probably faked. He appeared every bit the type to act his way out of a troubling situation.

"We know there was—let's just say," Jack explained, "an event with another man. We're currently running down a paternity test that should answer the question."

The senator's expression closed completely then.

"We have reason to believe the encounter was not a welcome one," Anne added without saying *the word*.

Despite his restraint, the man's face turned deathly pale. His eyes widened like saucers. She and Jack seemed to have that effect during interviews, even with someone as practiced at disguise as this man clearly was. Anne had to clutch the armrests of her chair to remain seated. She wanted to jump up and demand that he admit what he had done.

This man was somehow involved in what happened. Anne was sure of it.

"I've been reading her journal," she said, only at that moment deciding to share this information. He apparently had lost his ability to speak, at least momentarily. "I believe we're getting very close to uncovering evidence of the details she shared. Once we have what we need, I'm confident the murder case will be reopened. But this time, there will be a different defendant. My only regret is that I couldn't make that happen before she died in prison for a crime she did not commit."

The emotion that poured out of her with the revelations left her weak and on the verge of shaking. She should not have ignored her mother all those years. No matter that her mother had turned away her only attempts for a connection after high school, Anne should have kept trying. She should have fought for the truth. Regret and pain welled inside her so fast she could hardly breathe.

"I can understand your need to somehow make this right." Langston seemed to have gathered his wits once more. "But Mary is dead. What good can come of turning your own life upside down to find answers that likely will not change a thing?"

"She was innocent." Anne surprised herself by saying the words with strength and determination. "Her name should be cleared. She deserves—I deserve—the truth."

The senator inclined his head and studied her. "At what expense to you? In your line of work, reputation is everything. You need clients to trust you on all levels. It would be a shame to neglect your career for this futile endeavor."

Anne shook visibly with the impact of his words. Had he just threatened to damage her reputation? Clearly a US senator had the power to do such a thing. Also very clear was the idea that he had looked into her life.

"Particularly," Jack cut in, "if those rumors are false. I'm sure you felt the same way when Adrina Wilson made her allegations. Thankfully you were able to keep those out of the media for the most part—which is a major feat in itself these days."

The blood drained from Langston's face once more. "That," he said, his voice tight, "was a woman out to get something for nothing. I never touched her. She smelled money, and she wanted it." He snapped his mouth shut as if he'd only just realized that he wasn't supposed to speak of the matter.

So much for the nondisclosure agreement.

"But it was the other—the physical relationship," Anne suggested, "Adrina didn't want. Was that the true issue? Mary's journal reflects much the same. She didn't want what happened, and yet fear kept her from going to the proper authorities." She was really reaching here, but somehow she couldn't stop herself.

"This conversation is over." Langston stood. "I'm certain you can see yourselves out."

Anne and Jack rose from their chairs.

"Again," Jack said, "we appreciate your time. Would you let your assistant, Carin Wallace, know that we're trying to get in touch? I'm confident she has some of the answers we're looking for."

Langston remained silent. Fury burned red on his face, glowing in his eyes.

No one, not even the woman who had greeted them when they arrived, waited outside the office to escort them from the house. This surprised Anne. They walked along the marble-floored hall and into the grand foyer. No sign of Eve or an assistant or a member of the household staff.

Apparently the senator had wanted to ensure today's conversation was kept absolutely quiet.

Again, Jack checked the vehicle before they got in to leave. At the end of the driveway, they waited for the gates to open and rolled forward.

They had a new place to stay. Anne had taken care of that matter while they waited for their lunch at Judith's. If the woman had been in today, she hadn't come out to say hello. Maybe she couldn't bear to face Anne after what she'd done—filling Eve in on their conversation. But then perhaps Judith didn't realize she'd done exactly what they'd wanted her to do—spread the word they were here and looking for information.

"Our tail is back." Jack nodded toward the rearview mirror.

"Are we still going to shop?" She watched the black sedan in the side mirror.

"Why not. He can follow us there, and we'll

lose him after that. Just be prepared in case he makes some sort of aggressive move."

Vividly recalling yesterday's driving adventures, Anne leaned deeper into the seat, braced one hand on the door's armrest and the other on the console between them. "Got it."

The drive via US-14 from Barrington to Crystal Lake took all of five minutes. Another five or so minutes later and they arrived in the parking lot of the superstore they'd agreed upon.

Jack watched as the black sedan drove on past where they had parked. It wound through the lines of parked cars, finally sliding into a slot three rows away.

"I guess they want to know the location of our new hotel," Anne surmised. Motel actually. The one she'd chosen wasn't one those watching them would likely consider.

"We'll just have to make sure that doesn't happen."

They emerged from the car. Jack reached into the back seat and got the box. "Just in case." He looked at Anne over the top of the car.

"Good idea."

They walked together to the entrance. Anne had never shopped for clothes with a man. This would be a unique experience for sure. She grabbed a cart. Jack deposited the box in the cart, and she placed her shoulder bag on top of it.

"Ladies first," Jack suggested.

"Works for me." Anne headed for the women's department.

While she perused the racks of tops, Jack stepped a short distance away and made a call. She glanced at him from time to time, hoping there wasn't bad news. Or maybe this was a good call and she would have something better to think about instead of being frustrated over the meeting with Langston. What a jerk the man was.

The sound of her own cell phone vibrating tugged her attention to her purse. She poked around inside until she found it.

Lisa.

Worry sent a flare of adrenaline in her chest. "Hey, what's going on?"

"Hey, Anne. I hope I'm not catching you at a bad time."

"No." She rifled through the tops on the rack in front of her. "It's fine. Everything okay?"

"I'm not sure."

Her assistant did not sound okay. "What's going on?"

"The tile supplier just called about our new job. He said he'd forgotten about a customer on the list ahead of us who apparently wants the exact same tile we ordered for the principal bathroom."

Anne's stomach dipped. Not good. "What kind of delay are we looking at?"

"Two to three weeks from today. He claims the tile we ordered that will arrive next week will have to go to the other customer."

That kind of delay absolutely would not work.

"Hold on," Lisa said before Anne could respond. "Got another call."

Anne forced herself to focus on the task at hand despite the news from Lisa. She grabbed a mustard-colored tee without a logo or image plastered across the front. She tossed it into the cart and carried on sorting through the offerings on the rack. When the seconds continued to tick off, she glanced at the screen to ensure the call was still connected. It was and she was still on hold.

She hoped this was not more trouble. The idea that the timing was worrisome wasn't lost on her. Could Langston really work that fast? They'd only left the meeting a few minutes ago. Then again, he could have started this as soon as he heard she was in town.

A black tee caught her attention. Plain. Good. She plucked it from the rack and tossed it into the cart as well. Maybe one more, and that would be enough. She settled on a pale rose-colored one, and it joined the others in the cart. She glanced at Jack, who lingered close and still appeared to be in deep conversation on his own phone.

She grabbed two pairs of jeans and headed

for the lingerie department, which was next to this one. She glanced back to ensure Jack followed. He did, but thankfully he kept his distance while she grabbed the necessary bras and undies as well as a nightshirt.

All she needed now was a few toiletries like deodorant and a disposable razor. Maybe some mascara.

"Sorry!" Lisa said into her ear, making her jump. "You are really not going to believe this. It was the same guy—the tile supplier. Now he says the kitchen-floor tile is on back order. But I know it's not because I spoke to one of the guys who works there this morning to go over the suggested coordinating trim. It was not on back order, Anne. Something is going on with this guy. I mean, I can call around and see what I find out from other wholesalers, but this is very strange."

Anne's fingers tightened around the cart handle. Nothing she could do from here…except stay calm. "Just do what you can to ensure we have what we need to start in fourteen days."

"Don't worry," Lisa assured her. "I will. I just wanted you to know that something weird is happening here."

"I'm sorry for the trouble, Lisa. I promise there will be a big bonus in this one."

Lisa laughed. "I got you. Don't worry. Bonus or not, this is going to get done."

Anne thanked her and ended the call. She tossed her phone back into her bag. Outrage rushed through her veins, and she wanted to scream. How the hell had he done this so fast? Even if he'd started yesterday...this was incredibly quick. His statements in the meeting suggested he had already done a background search on her. But the details of her latest client's contract? That was over the top.

Well, of course he had gotten in-depth information. He was rich and powerful...and a scumbag.

How much money did it take, she mused, to turn longtime suppliers against her?

"Everything okay?"

Jack must have noticed the look on her face because he was suddenly beside her.

"I don't know. It seems we have a problem with our tile supplier." She looked directly at Jack, hoping he would read the innuendo in her eyes. "This morning all was well with our orders, and now suddenly there are delays. I want to believe this has nothing to do with what's going on here..." She moved her head side to side. "But after that veiled threat he made about my life, I'm not so sure."

Her phone sounded the warning that she had a new text message. She grabbed it from her bag and stared at the screen.

You will not believe this!

Her heart dropping, she opened the text box.

There may be a snag with our permit for the job!!!

Anne typed a quick message letting Lisa know to call if she couldn't get it straightened out.

"And now—" she looked at Jack "—there's a holdup on our permit."

"Now, that one," he said, his own frustration showing, "I would put money on being prompted by a call from someone on the senator's personal staff."

Anne was angrier than she had been in…she couldn't remember when. She forced the worries aside. "We heading to the men's department now?"

"Yeah. Let's get this done and get out of here."

They started that way, and then she realized she hadn't asked him about his call.

"Everything okay on your end?"

"My call was all good." He flashed her a grin.

She liked his smiles, and she was immensely thankful he hadn't laid another issue at her feet. "We'll need to stop at health and beauty aids too."

"Deodorant," he noted with a nod.

"For sure."

Unlike her, he was quick with his shopping. They even swung through the aisle where camping supplies were sold and grabbed another flashlight and batteries. Then after a quick stroll through Health and Beauty, they were off to the checkout lanes. Once they were checked out and ready to go, rather than walk out the main exit, he ushered her in a different direction.

"Where are we going?"

He flashed her another of those adorable grins. "To the garden department."

The garden department was on the opposite end of the enormous superstore from where they had parked. She wasn't sure how that would help, but obviously the man had a plan. To her surprise, she trusted him completely.

As they reached the area stocked with all manner of grilling and pool supplies as well as loads of plants, he checked his cell and continued toward the exit.

Outside a car waited at the pedestrian crosswalk. Jack opened the rear passenger door for her. She climbed in, her bag of goods in hand, and he slid in next to her, the box and his own bag in tow.

"All set?" the driver asked.

"We are. If you don't mind, go out on this end of the lot."

"Will do."

Jack turned to her. "Uber," he whispered. "He's taking us to the car-rental center. We'll pick up our new car and head to our hotel."

Anne twisted around in the seat and looked for the black sedan that had parked just beyond the grocery entrance—all the way at the other end of the massive building.

Then she grinned at Jack. "That was good." Worry tugged her lips into a frown. "What about your car?"

"Someone from the agency will pick it up."

Anne relaxed and settled back into the seat. She was grateful to be in such good hands. She just hoped he was good enough to keep this search for the truth from turning into a bigger nightmare.

Though she hated admitting as much, she hadn't expected her business and certainly not her life to be in danger while pursuing this quest.

But then, she hadn't fully embraced the idea that Mary—her mother—had been telling the truth.

And that someone would be willing to do anything to prevent that truth from coming out.

Chapter Thirteen

Moody Motel
Carpenter Street, 6:00 p.m.

The place wasn't as bad as Anne had feared. Not that Jack had given her any particular specifications regarding where to book a room. Still, she sort of wanted him to be pleased, if not impressed, with her choice. The place was far from impressive, but that wasn't the primary requirement this go-around.

There had been two rooms with a connecting door available. The motel was not an upscale place by any stretch of the imagination. The upside was that the rooms were clean. A little shabby, but in a charming sort of way. The outside had been painted recently in one of those popular dark bluish-black colors. The inside was freshly painted in a very pale shade of gray. No carpet. Hardwood and tile. The tiny bathroom was, to be kind, vintage—including a clawfoot tub.

Anne liked it. She wasn't sure how Jack felt. He

was probably accustomed to staying in the higher-end hotels. Her goal had been to find a decent place where no one would look—at least not at first.

This was, she figured, exactly that sort of place.

It was funny, she considered as she hung up her new clothes in the very tiny closet, how easily appeased she was with accommodations. She went to great lengths to provide beautiful, elegant and trending designs to her clients. Personally, if she didn't work from home, she would live in a little cottage by the water somewhere. Vintage was her favorite style. But clients expected certain things when they met with a designer. So she lived in an upscale neighborhood in a trendy town house that would hopefully whet their appetites and earn their trust.

Her hands fell to her sides. At university one of her professors had warned that she shouldn't be afraid to color outside the lines. He'd done this because she never took risks with her designs. She was very good, he had insisted, but she needed to extend outside her boundaries. Over time her work had grown and taken on more of a cutting edge. But her personal life—the person she was—stayed in that *safe* zone.

Which probably explained how she'd almost reached thirty with few romantic relationships.

It wasn't that she didn't try. She did. She just didn't try very hard…or often.

Her gaze swung to the connecting door. Jack kind of made her want to jump outside that safe zone she'd built around her personal life. It was easy to imagine coloring outside the lines with him.

She shook her head. He was here to do a job, not become a romantic interest for a lonely designer about to hit the big 3-0.

A knock on the connecting door made her jump.

She pressed a hand to her chest and sucked in the breath that had deserted her. Squaring her shoulders, she walked to the door and opened it. Better to keep her head out of those dreamy places.

He smiled. He really had the nicest smile. Nice lips too. Great eyes. Anne almost sighed out loud. She chased away the thoughts.

"What's up?" She was tired...mentally and physically. Not herself. It wasn't like her to fantasize about random men. Not that there was really anything at all random about this one. *Enough, Anne!*

"I thought I'd order dinner in. Have it delivered since there's no restaurant on the property."

She frowned. "I know this place is kind of low end. I hope it's okay. I figured it wouldn't be somewhere they would consider—at least not the first place on their list anyway." She laughed at herself. "I may have read too many mystery novels."

He chuckled. "It was a good choice. Really."

"Thanks." She relaxed a little. "So...food. What did you have in mind?"

"Chinese? Mexican? Mediterranean? Regular old American? There's quite a list who deliver."

"Chinese. Pick a variety of things, and we'll share." Immediately the image of her using chopsticks to feed him came to mind. She banished it. She so had to get her head on straight. Maybe it was the stress. Had to be.

"Another good choice." He tapped the screen of his cell phone and started the process.

She left him in the doorway between their rooms and went back to unbagging her purchases. It was either that or stare at his perfect profile while he ordered their dinner. *Strange behavior, Anne.* Apparently digging into her mother's sad love story was getting to her...making her desperate.

That had to be it. Otherwise, what in the world had her suddenly daydreaming about an encounter with the man assigned to investigate her case? She decided it was that age-old problem of needing to take her mind off her troubles. Hadn't she learned that in Psych 101 back during her freshman year of college?

Either that or the other age-old suggestion that

barreling toward thirty had her biological clock acting up. At this point she hadn't even considered children.

No. Stop it.

She'd been dateless for ages now. Hadn't been kissed or hugged by a man in months—maybe a year. She groaned. Pretty pathetic. But no reason to go all desperate and sex crazed. She wandered to the bathroom to stash her necessities. With no room on the tiny sink, she lined them up on the toilet tank lid.

She considered the tub. She loved its curves and the deeper depth. Maybe she'd have a soak later. She needed to relax, and a leisurely bath might just do the trick. Get her mind off the ancient history of an abandoned baby and the present dilemma of a lonely woman.

Her eyes rolled. Pathetic.

Back in her room, Jack waited at the shared door, one broad shoulder braced against the doorframe. Could he not look so…sexy? Another groan welled inside her, but she tamped it down.

"Thirty-to-forty minutes," he announced.

"Thanks."

She stood there a moment, uncertain what to do. Maybe he'd say something, get a conversation going about the investigation. Otherwise, her mounting tension would continue. She was obviously going through something, and it was ridiculous. She was no teenager, and this was no game.

"You handling today okay? I know some of it wasn't exactly comfortable."

She lifted one shoulder and let it fall, fixed her attention on the events of the day. "I had this idea of how things would go." She dropped onto the foot of the bed—thankfully the mattress seemed fairly comfortable. "But I was way off in my assumptions."

"You thought—" he stepped into her space, pulled the chair from the small desk and took a seat "—you'd find the same thing the detective did. You'd feel you had done your due diligence, and then you could go home and put this all behind you."

Wow. He was a mind reader too.

"Something like that."

"Assuming the most complicated situation or ending isn't the route our minds usually take." He braced his forearms on his thighs. "But sometimes that's just where life takes us."

She tried to ignore how their knees almost touched. The room was so small the end of the bed was only about three or four feet from the desk and the connecting door. But she wasn't complaining. His nearness was comforting. It made her feel warm and safe. Gave her the courage to keep her chin up and her shoulders square in this situation so alien to her. Her only experience with this sort of thing was the occasional true crime documentary.

"I thought I knew what happened. The woman who gave birth to me killed the man who fathered me. For reasons I would likely never know or understand." She shook her head. "She'd never written to me. Wouldn't see me when I tried to visit her. I assumed she never wanted me—the same story some of my foster mothers told me while they were pointing out how happy I should be to have what they provided. Which wasn't always what a child needed."

"I get that your childhood wasn't what it should have been." His eyes searched hers. "But you rose above it. You've done really well for yourself. You have every reason to be proud of your accomplishments. If your mother knew anything about your life, I'm sure she was proud as well."

"Thank you. I hope so. I haven't really worried about what she thought since I was a kid, but I would be lying if I didn't say my feelings have changed. This whole endeavor has certainly been eye opening." She glanced at the journal that lay on her bed. She'd taken it out of the box with the intention of reviewing certain entries. "When I read the journal, I wasn't convinced of anything beyond what I already felt. Not really. I mean anyone can write words on a page. Everyone has their story. I had little confidence that her story would prove accurate to any real degree. Maybe it was what she believed to be the truth… but that's not always the same as the real truth."

But she had begun to see the full picture now. Her gaze settled on the man watching her. About many things—like her own story. The way she ignored her personal needs. How she pretended work was everything and that there was no time for anything else.

Slow down, girl.

"I, as well as the team at the agency, fully believe that Mary was innocent. I personally am confident that what we've heard so far confirms as much."

Anne crossed her legs in an effort to get more comfortable. Her foot nudged his shin, and she uncrossed and then recrossed in the other direction. "Sorry."

"No problem—I'm the one who's crowding you." He shifted a little.

"It's fine. Really." *Focus on the case!* Deep breath. "Do you think there's any chance Adrina Wilson would talk to me?" If the senator had taken advantage of his assistant, that would make believing he'd done the same to Mary far easier to accept for anyone hearing the story.

"It's doubtful. She signed an NDA. She would be setting herself up for serious legal repercussions if she did."

Anne had thought as much, but it never hurt to get a second opinion. "The fact that he paid her to sign this agreement suggests he was guilty, right?"

"Most people see it that way. There's always the possibility that even if he was innocent of the charge he didn't want to deal with being trashed in the media. Like you, I see the agreement as hush money for his crossing the line. How far over that line he went" he shrugged "—who knows. I will say that this business with Wilson was ten years ago—just as he was assuming his current office, so keeping negative reports out of the media was more important than ever."

She supposed that was a valid point.

"Thirty years ago," he went on, "Langston was younger and had far less to lose. I'm guessing he wasn't worried about Mary coming forward. She had to protect her reputation as a teacher of young children, and she was engaged to be married. She had everything to lose at the time, and he had basically nothing to worry about. It was her word against his. No matter who their friends and colleagues believed, the damage would be done to Mary's reputation."

A very smart analysis. Not a fair conclusion,

but the most likely one that would have been reached at the time. Jack was really good at his job. Handsome, charming, kind and smart. Why was it that she never ran into a guy like him in her everyday life? Would she have even noticed?

Not fair, she decided. She no doubt ran into really nice men often, but she ignored them. Her attention was more often than not on work. The truth was if she didn't put herself out there, she didn't have to worry about being hurt. Relationships and marriage led to other things like children and...

It was difficult to see going down that road after the childhood she'd had.

As much as she hated blaming so much on her childhood, her inability to take the usual relationship risks was a direct result of those early years. On some level she understood that this moment—this time with Jack—was temporary and less risky maybe. In the end they would go their own ways. No real jeopardy involved when the relationship was temporary, right?

She had lost her mind. With a deep breath, she dismissed the thoughts and concentrated on what they were here to do. "I feel like the things we've learned from Mrs. Farrell and then about the position at BioTech lends credibility to Mary's claims. I don't know if finding that lab she used will tell us anything about who, besides Neil, might have been my father, but the idea that she was worried is a potential motive for the other person involved. It's proof of the involvement of a third party. Someone who could have committed the murder to shut her up and/or to protect himself."

"You're right about that. Even if it's best not to attempt a meeting with Wilson, we still have Carin Carter Wallace to locate. She has stayed under the radar a lot. There has to be a reason for that."

Anne had pondered the idea as well. "When you look at the time frame that she went to work for Langston, it was not long before he took higher office and only a few months after her husband died. Do you think she had decided to come back and demand some sort of compensation for the secret she'd kept all those years? At that point, she didn't have to worry about her husband learning whatever secrets she had. He was dead."

"You might not be far off in your assessment. Carin married a wealthy investor after leaving her life here behind. He was a good deal older than her, and he'd been married before. When he died her inheritance was a pittance compared to what his grown children received. There was likely a prenup, so she couldn't exactly contest it with any hope of winning. I'm guessing she was ready to move on to the next option for living the good life."

Anne contemplated the idea. "We still don't know the reason Carin left in the first place. She may have seen or heard something that put her in a position to be concerned for her safety. Getting out of here may have felt like the safest thing to do at the time. But after the murder, she realized she had a sort of insurance policy that would protect her, but she didn't come back because she'd already met her rich widower."

Jack smiled. "Exactly. You're a natural at this. You sure you don't want to change careers?"

She laughed. "Whether I'm good at this or not—which remains to be seen—I love what I do."

"You're very good at what you do." He made a *what can I say* face. "I checked out your website. Perused your gallery." He flashed that smile again. "Tell me about your plans for the future. Beyond all this, I mean."

"My plan is to keep building my business—which is why this big client with the tile issues… and now the permit glitch—is so important." She thought about all the things she envisioned for the future. "I have this five-year plan I hope takes us—my assistant, Lisa, and me—to the next level. I'll get an office in downtown Aurora, and I'd like to buy one of the amazing historic homes and make it mine." She rolled her eyes. "I'm sure you're wishing you hadn't asked."

The way he was watching her she felt certain she'd over answered the question. Good grief, she'd never had such trouble in a man's presence. One of her best business assets was her ability to keep her cool in the most stressful situation. Then again, this wasn't business.

"You're not going to believe this." Jack reached into his pocket for his cell phone. "I'm renovating this nineteenth-century Victorian on Augusta Street in Oak Park."

Stunned, Anne accepted his phone and swiped through the photos. The house was perfect. The wood floors looked very salvageable. The walls appeared to be in good shape. It was exactly the sort of home she hoped to have one day.

"It's great. I'd love to hear your plans. Are you remodeling or restoring?"

His fingers brushed hers as he took the phone from her hand. Heat shot up her arm. She tried to stifle the gasp but didn't quite accomplish her mission.

"I want to restore as much as possible." He ignored or was hopefully oblivious to her reaction. "I'll save the remodeling for areas like the kitchen, where a more modern update is most convenient."

"Good plan." She managed a smile, no matter that the way he studied her now was deeply unsettling…in a good way. She leaned forward slightly, unable to drag her gaze from his.

He stared at her lips. "The food should be here…"

Her breath foolishly caught again. He had to know she was attracted to him. God, she was so embarrassed.

"I'm sorry." She drew away slightly. "I guess I was so caught up in our conversation I…" She shook her head. "Sorry."

He sat his phone on the desk without taking his eyes off her, then he reached out, gently traced the outline of her cheek with the tips of his fingers. Desire ignited inside her, and her heart started to pound.

He dropped his hand away. "I should be the one to apologize. I couldn't stop staring at you, and I shouldn't have let myself get carried away."

"Please," she urged, her voice barely a whisper, "get carried away some more."

He leaned closer, brushed his lips across hers. "I can do that," he murmured against the lips he had set on fire. Then he kissed her again, softly, slowly.

She put her arms around his neck and leaned into the kiss. Oh, how she wanted to feel this… this fire and anticipation.

A pounding on his door tore them apart.

"The food," he said hoarsely. He turned back to her, licked his lips hungrily. "To be continued."

He walked out of the room.

Anne braced her elbows on her knees and plunked her face into her hands. What was she thinking? This was not supposed to happen. She forced her lungs to fill with air. Not smart. Not smart.

She stood. To heck with smart! Her fingers fumbled as she quickly unfastened the buttons of her blouse—the one she'd been wearing this morning, which saved it from the fire. She tore it off and reached for the waist of her pants.

Jack came back into the room carrying bags of food. He stalled, stared at the blouse on the floor and then her.

She shrugged, her fingers still clutching her waistband. "I thought we could eat later…after we do the to-be-continued part."

He placed the bags on the desk and moved toward her.

Her heart thumped so hard she couldn't catch her breath.

And then he kissed her, his hands roving over her bare back until he found the place where her bra fastened.

Her body melted against him. No more thinking.

Chapter Fourteen

Journal Entry
Thirty Years Ago
August 10

This was the worst that could have happened.

No, not the worst. But close. The position Neil had wanted so badly was stolen by a friend. He was devastated, and I was devastated for him.

The so-called friend who stole it was a year ahead of Neil. He had graduated in May. Not at the top of his class either as Neil was set to do. No, he was mediocre at best. So far he'd taken his bar exam multiple times without passing it.

He was no Neil, and the company had made a huge mistake choosing the other man over Neil.

I wanted to scream then, still do now whenever I think about it.

No matter that I preferred he didn't go with that company, it was unfair.

At the time Eve was still avoiding me, which was just as well. I wanted nothing to do with her or her lowlife fiancé. Carin hadn't returned. I wondered if she did come back whether she would take Eve's side in all that had happened. At that point I didn't trust anyone to be who they claimed to be. How could Neil and I have been friends with those two for so long and not have seen the duplicity they were capable of?

I knew then that I would never forgive them. Never.

I wish I could have told Neil about the other, but I feared there would be terrible repercussions. The worry there would be physical violence if he ever learned what had happened was a true concern. Although Neil and I didn't have a gun in the house, I felt as if he would get one if he learned that awful truth. I could never tell him. It was better if he didn't know. We just had to move on with our lives and not look back. The law firm in Crystal Lake had been pushing hard to have Neil come on board when he graduated. It was a reputable, long-standing firm. The offer was a generous one. There was no reason not to take it. The potential for the big leagues wasn't as great, but it would work. As long as we had each other, what else really mattered?

I was certain I would feel much better when all of that was behind us. I had a terrible feeling about it. I recognized that we couldn't trust the people we thought were our friends. And I also understood that they would never want the things I knew to be revealed. Everyone had their secrets. Some more than others, and the knowledge of those secrets made me very nervous.

I made the decision to focus on the future and pretend I didn't know what those evil so-called friends were capable of. School was about to start back, so that would occupy much of my time. I had you to get ready for the baby and the wedding. Neil had finally agreed to something far more low-key. I was glad because I just wanted to be happy and settled and not draw a lot of attention to ourselves. It sounds strange, I know, but I thought I needed to stay very small so they would ignore me and the things I knew.

I read once that the universe gives back to you what you put out to it. With that in mind, I focused on being extra kind to all. I thought good thoughts most of the time. I had hoped that attitude would get me through until we were safe again.

Apparently I was wrong to assume the threat to us would just go away.

I wish I didn't have to be so cryptic as I write this. I would very much like to spell out all that I know for sure. That would make finding the rest much easier. But I don't dare. I'm in prison, so nothing—not even my body—is private and certainly not safe.

I have to be careful...and should you ever take up this challenge to find the truth, you should be very careful too.

Chapter Fifteen

Crystal Lake
Saturday, July 12
Jones Residence
Maplewood Lane, 9:30 a.m.

Anne had expected breakfast to be awkward.

Jack had already been up and in the shower in his room when she woke up. There were no adequate words for how relieved she was that she had been alone in her own room when she woke. Not that there had been a single regret—at least on her part, but she'd felt a little embarrassed. Her neediness had been more than obvious, and he'd been so attentive…and so amazing.

Trying not to swoon with the memories, she had taken a shower—though she had wanted a long hot soak so badly—and hurriedly dried her hair. She had chosen to wear the black tee. It felt weird wearing jeans that hadn't been washed, but there was no way to change that now. Since she'd forgotten to grab a pair of sneakers at the store, she was stuck with wearing the loafers. They were fairly comfortable, but she was a sneakers girl.

Then Jack had knocked on the connecting door, and she'd been dazed and out of sorts just seeing him. They had stopped for breakfast at a local diner. He'd carried the conversation as they'd eaten. She had managed the occasional nod or hummed agreement. Then they'd gotten back into the rental car and driven to Barrington to see if Carin Carter Wallace was home.

Whoever answered the intercom at the gate had said she wasn't, so from there they'd driven back to Crystal Lake to the home of Detective Harlan Jones.

Anne suspected he would not be happy about their visit on a Saturday morning, but she was immensely thankful for diving directly into the investigation. Even at breakfast, Jack had kept the conversation focused on what they had discovered so far and what he hoped to accomplish going forward.

The prospect of potentially discussing last night had been terrifying. It had been so long since she'd dealt with a morning after, and she felt completely off balance.

Not that it hadn't been awesome, she considered again. It was completely amazing. Jack had made her experience things she had not known were possible. She'd lost count of the times he had made her...well, feel really, really good.

The first thing she'd wanted to do this morning was to call Lisa and tell her all about it. Except she couldn't with him in the next room and the connecting door ajar. Not to mention that talking about it to another person would equate to it being real. Last night had not been real—as in some sort of declaration of a personal connection or the start of a relationship.

It was just something that happened at the end of the day between two people involved in an intense situation.

That was it. No big deal.

Except she still felt warm inside this morning. She felt...

Stop. The fact was that they were together because of his job. It wasn't about anything personal. When the investigation concluded he would go back to Chicago and she would go home...to work.

Funny how the work she loved suddenly felt lacking.

Just stop.

Jack parked in the driveway behind an SUV. Next to the SUV was a fishing boat. Nothing large or elaborate, just a flat-bottom boat with a small motor sitting atop a trailer. A man who matched the online images of Detective Jones placed a cooler in the boat and then a pair of fishing rods. His weekend plans appeared to include fishing. Hopefully that meant he was in a good mood. This was another cold call. The detective might or might not talk to them. Particularly if he figured out they were looking into one of his old cases.

Anne mentally crossed her fingers and turned to the man behind the wheel. "Looks like he's home."

"And perhaps in a good mood." Jack smiled, and her pulse reacted.

She was so overreacting to last night. "I was thinking the same thing."

They got out of the car at the same time. He glanced across the top of the rental at her and gave her a nod as if he understood she was a little nervous. She was. This interview would be a bit touchier than the others, and she needed to be on her toes. This man was a cop—the one who investigated the murder thirty years ago. He was retired now, but that didn't mean he would want to admit mistakes. Though thirty years older than the images from the newspaper clippings in Mary's box of saved things, the man had stayed fit. His dark hair was sprinkled with gray now, and the beard was new. He wore jeans and a tee and sneakers. He was ready for his weekend… and they were stepping into his path.

Harlan Jones stared at them as they approached. He braced one hand on the boat and with the other reached up and adjusted his glasses. Those were new too. "Good morning."

"Good morning, Mr. Jones," Jack responded. "I'm Jack Brenner, and this is Anne Griffin." She forced her lips into a smile.

The man with fishing on his mind narrowed his gaze, looked them each over. "If you're here to preach to me, don't waste your breath," he warned. "Or if you're here selling something, I'm a retired police detective, which means I live on a budget, so don't waste your time."

"Fair enough." Jack nodded. "Actually, I'm from the Colby Agency—a private investigations firm in Chicago."

The detective's head went up in acknowledgment. "I've heard of the Colby Agency. What brings you to my home?"

Anne was surprised he hadn't already gotten wind of their endeavor. Maybe retirement meant he'd lost touch with the local grapevine.

"We're looking into the Neil Reed murder."

Surprise flared in his eyes. "Talk about an old one. I'm surprised anyone even remembers the case."

"Mary Morton was my mother," Anne explained, finally finding her footing. "She passed away recently."

The former detective's surprise was overtaken by the guard that went up. His expression closed. All signs of what he was thinking or feeling vanished.

"She left a journal," Jack said, "and we're looking into some of the allegations she made about others involved in the events leading up to and including the murder of Reed."

The former detective's jaw tightened, but to his credit, Mr. Jones didn't make a run for the house. "I haven't heard about the case being reopened."

"That's coming, I suspect." Jack surveyed the man's boat. "Looks as if you have your day planned out."

Jones nodded. "I fish every chance I get. It's my favorite thing to do. Thirty-five-plus years as a cop... I figure I earned all the fishing I can get in before old age takes over."

"Law enforcement takes a toll," Jack agreed. "Would you have a few minutes for a couple of questions?"

He looked from Jack to Anne, then shrugged. "I suppose so. Shoot."

Anne was still stuck on the words *That's coming*. Did Jack really believe their—his—investigation could make that happen? The official reopening of the case? Once more she felt as if her head was spinning. Not that she didn't want the case reopened. She did. She just had been skeptical and… Wow, this might really be happening. *Pay attention to the now, Anne!*

"There was never any determination about where the weapon came from." Jack went straight for one of the bigger missing elements of the investigation.

"The ballistics didn't match anything we had on file," Jones admitted. "There was no 4473—firearms transaction record—submitted for Morton or Reed, so we can only assume the weapon was purchased illegally. No one we interviewed was aware the couple owned a firearm. However they came into possession of that gun, her prints were the only ones on it."

Anne spoke up, "But she said in her statement that she picked up the gun from where it lay on the floor when she found Neil. She had no idea where it came from or who fired it. Most anyone would have done the same thing. It's instinct to pick up and inspect something unexpected found in your home."

He nodded. "That's what she said, but I wasn't buying it." He turned his hands up. "I get that she was your mother, but she had blood on her clothes, and she was the only person seen coming in or out of the house around the time of the murder."

"There was no gun powder residue on her

hands," Jack pointed out. "As for the blood, it was smeared on her clothes from trying to render emergency care to the man she loved. There was no blood splatter pattern from standing close when the weapon fired and the bullet hit him in the chest."

"We're confident she washed her hands and forearms," Jones countered. "Morton was smart. She knew what to do and what to say. Her story about picking up the gun before we even asked felt too accommodating and detailed for someone overcome with emotion. As for the blood, a splatter pattern couldn't be found after she smeared blood over it. She made sure of it. Besides, no one else had motive—not like her anyway. And she was the one to find him. It was all just a little too convenient."

"What about her friend, Eve Langston—Redford at the time?" Fury simmered inside Anne. So this was what her mother had been up against. "She was seen in the neighborhood that day, according to one of the neighbors you interviewed."

"It's possible the neighbor who saw her," Jack added, "got the time wrong."

Anne wished that neighbor was still alive. It would have been helpful to hear directly from her.

Mr. Jones laughed. "The senator's wife? I

can't imagine what motive she would have had to murder her best friend's husband." He sent a pointed look at Jack. "I do know how to conduct a homicide investigation, you know."

There it was. No more Mr. Nice Guy.

"First," Anne argued, "he wasn't a senator at the time, and Eve wasn't his wife until later. So neither of those scenarios had anything to do with what happened." Her gaze narrowed on the man. "I'm guessing," she went on, trying not to let her irritation show, "you didn't consider Eve's husband, Kevin, as a person of interest either. No matter that he'd just stolen a position with BioTech that had been offered to Neil. I can't imagine that wouldn't be considered motive."

Anne wanted to toss in the possible sexual-assault allegation she'd learned about and the paternity test...but Mrs. Farrell was right. It would only make her mother look guiltier. As for the previous sexual-assault allegation involving Adrina Wilson, surely any good cop would have dug up that one.

Then again, she wasn't sure this man fit the definition of a good cop.

The former detective actually laughed this time. "She really pulled out all the stops in that journal, didn't she? The fact is Kevin Langston could not have killed Neil Reed any more than his future wife could have because they were having drinks together in town at the time of the murder. Their alibi was confirmed."

"I noticed that in the file," Jack commented. "But the location and the person who verified their alibi weren't named."

Jones held up his hands in a signal of surrender. "That one is on me. I must have failed to list those items. They were at JJ's, and the owner, Jerry Trenton, confirmed their alibi." He dropped his hands to his sides. "The truth is it was crystal clear who the shooter was. The rest was just a matter of filling in the blanks."

Anne required a moment to ride out the shock of that news. No wonder Judith had gone straight to Eve about Anne and Jack's visit. Her ex-husband had been the Langstons' alibi. Oh, how the plot thickened.

"You're saying," Anne pressed, her anger stirring once more, "that you were so certain my mother killed my father that you really didn't consider anyone else."

The detective's hands went to his hips then, and he glared at her, his face hard with his own rising anger. "I did not say that. I looked at several other persons of interest. The fact is, lady, Mary Morton killed him. End of story. As sad as that might make you, it's the truth."

Anne wasn't a cop but she found it suspicious that he could remember all these details so well thirty years later. More likely, someone had spoken to him already. Made sure he remembered all the right answers.

"You never mentioned a motive," Jack said, dragging the guy's attention to him. "What was her motive for killing the man she intended to marry…the father of her unborn child? Any way I look at it, I can't find how doing so helped her in the slightest. He had no life insurance. You and I both know that for a young woman—a pregnant one—with no history of violence to suddenly obtain a weapon illegally and then shoot and kill the man she loved takes a strong motive. If there was nothing for her to gain, why did she do it? You found no evidence he'd cheated on her. No evidence of any sort of abuse. Nothing. That's a stretch, Detective."

Jones face lined with rage, he snapped, "I guess you had to be there. You had to see the lack of emotion when she was found hovering over his body. The dull, lifeless look in her eyes while I questioned her. The methodical, almost rehearsed answers."

"Did you consider that she was pregnant and emotionally devastated?" Jack argued. "What you're describing could easily have been shock."

The detective laughed, shook his head. "We can debate this all day, but I was there. I know what I saw and heard. She was guilty, and the case was closed."

"Did you interview Michael Smith to find out why he chose Langston for the position at his company after already making a deal with Reed?" Jack demanded next.

"I didn't see the point."

"What about Carin Carter Wallace?" Anne demanded. "She took off just before the murder. She was friends with Mary and Neil as well as Eve and Kevin. She's the senator's personal assistant now. Has been for years. You found nothing suspicious about any of their activities? Never considered that close friends might know things useful to your investigation?"

His eyebrows lifted at her sarcastic tone. "Carter was not in Crystal Lake at the time of the murder. Her fiancé confirmed she was at home in Chicago. Even though she visited for a couple of days after the murder, she didn't hang around long."

"You didn't put that in the file either," Jack noted.

The man exhaled a big, put upon breath. "Looking back, I can see where I didn't do several things I would have done later on. Experience changes how you do things. I still had a lot to learn thirty years ago."

"I'm glad you mentioned that," Jack said.

"Why were you put on the case, considering your lack of experience at the time?"

Another of those impatient exhales from the former detective. "It was Labor Day weekend. Everyone else was on vacation. I was low man on the seniority roster, so I got stuck on call. Once the case was mine, I wasn't giving it up. I figured a big case like that would help set my career. I may not have documented everything exactly as I should have, but I guarantee you it all got done and the killer went to jail. End of story."

"And as it turned out, considering the lack of actual evidence or motive," Anne countered, disbelief and no small amount of frustration twisting inside her, "all the judge and jury needed for the Reed murder case was your testimony in the courtroom. That's astonishing."

When he would have argued Anne's point, Jack cut him off. "The fact that no one was assigned to ensure the new kid on the block covered all the bases in the investigation kind of makes you wonder," he suggested, "if someone involved with the murder had a friend in the department."

His own frustration tightened the detective's features, but rather than argue he hitched his head toward his boat. "The morning's wasting. I'm heading to the lake. If you have a complaint or any more questions, take it up with the chief."

When they were in the car driving away, Anne had gone way past frustration and into pure anger. "Did you buy any of that?"

"Parts, to some degree," he said, surprising her. But then he braked at an intersection and shifted his attention to her. "Detective Jones did what he was told to do. Anyone who has worked with the police understands that when there's a murder—particularly in a fairly small town like this one—a detective on vacation can be called in. No one wanted this case, so they handed it off to the rookie. Any potential mistakes would be his."

Anne's frustration and anger fizzled. "He wasn't important enough to protect."

"Or," Jack said as he took a right, "someone higher up was protecting the future senator and wanted a scapegoat in place in case someone ever came along and pointed out the holes in the investigation."

"Like us." Anne hadn't thought of that one. "Kevin Langston might have had a friend in the department making sure he was never dragged into the fray."

"I would put money on it." Jack flashed her a smile.

Her heart skipped a beat. "How do we go about finding out who that is—was?"

"After the conversation we just had with

Jones, I don't think we'll have to do anything except wait. Whoever decided how that investigation was to be handled will catch up with us."

In light of the fire at the hotel, the idea made Anne more than a little nervous and at the same time incredibly giddy.

She suspected the next couple of days were going to get even more interesting.

Chapter Sixteen

Barrington
Langston Residence
Plum Tree Road, 1:00 p.m.

Since the meeting with Detective Jones, Jack had driven to Carin Carter Wallace's residence on Rollings Hills Drive. Again that disembodied voice on the intercom at the gate had insisted Ms. Wallace was not home and she had no idea where she was this morning. *Personal time*, her calendar showed. He and Anne had simply shaken their heads. The woman was still avoiding them. No surprise really.

Since he felt confident the detective would make it a point to get word to the Langstons, Jack had decided that watching their home would be the right step. Anne had agreed. If Detective Jones was quick about it, one or both Langstons would likely be reacting sooner rather than later.

"If either one leaves the house—" Anne broke

the extended silence "—we're going to follow, right?"

"We are." They had grabbed lunch and spent some time surveilling the Wallace house to no avail. Jack had attempted to start a conversation from time to time, but nothing stuck. More than once he had considered bringing up last night, but there hadn't been a moment that felt right.

No, that wasn't true. If he were honest with himself, he worried that he'd read far too much into the moment. He wasn't at all sure she had felt the same way he had. She'd experienced the need and the urgency—that part had been obvious. But he wasn't sure she felt the deeper attraction, the deeper connection that he had. He liked Anne. A lot. And he wanted to know her better…if she was interested.

Since she hadn't brought up the subject either, taking her lead seemed like the right move. No matter that he actually wanted to talk about it. Part of him wanted to apologize for making the first move. He should have restrained himself. But the need to kiss her had overridden his senses. He'd had no choice. After that, there had been no stopping.

Not that he regretted what they'd shared. No way. He just hoped she didn't.

Last night had been…nice. In truth, it was way better than nice. Even *great* didn't feel like an adequate description. The best way to describe it was that he wanted it to happen again... and again after that.

Still, he had crossed a line no matter that he refused to regret any aspect of it. He cared about this woman, and he wanted to spend more time with her...if she was agreeable, and last night it had felt like she was.

But he wasn't pushing the idea. She was vulnerable right now. He'd lost control last night, but if it happened again, she would have to make the first move.

"You shouldn't feel guilty about last night."

Her words yanked him back to the here and now. Surprised him. He turned to her. "Why would you think I feel guilty?"

She kept her attention focused forward. "Well, I...you haven't mentioned it, and..."

He laughed softly. "I was waiting for you to bring it up." He studied her profile, easily spotted the uncertainty and hesitation there now that he looked more closely. She was nervous. "Since you brought it up, let me assure you that guilt is not what I feel."

She met his gaze then, hers wide. "I hope you don't regret it either. It was as much my decision as yours."

He shook his head. "No regret. As long as you have no guilt or regret..."

"No regret and no guilt. I'm glad it happened. It was really..." She closed her eyes, took a breath. "It was amazing and..." She looked directly into his eyes then. "I hope when this is finished, we can do it again." She snapped her eyes shut and winced. "I mean..."

"I think I know what you mean." He took her hand in his and set his attention on the property just up the block from where they were parked. This thing between them would have to wait until his work on the case was done.

She relaxed and he did the same, then her fingers curled around his.

He was glad she trusted him and, it seemed, she liked him. He was glad about that part as well.

Putting too much stock in a relationship that developed during an intense situation was not smart. And maybe this wasn't the brightest move he'd made. But he was in for however long it lasted.

Before he could get too lost in those thoughts, the gate to the Langston home started to swing open.

"Here we go." He sat up straighter, put both hands on the steering wheel.

Beside him, Anne leaned slightly forward in anticipation of who would be leaving the Langston residence.

The sleek black Mercedes that Eve Langston drove rolled forward. She took a right out of her driveway, and Jack caught a glimpse of the woman in the driver's side window. One of their targets was on the move.

Once the Mercedes was farther down the block, Jack eased onto the street and followed.

Tension coiled inside him along with the hope that the woman would meet with someone or do something that gave them the upper hand in this investigation. What they had right now was a lot of interesting and potentially case-altering scenarios but no evidence to back it up. Not unlike what Detective Jones had when the case was originally investigated. Other than the proverbial smoking gun, he'd had nothing that proved Mary Morton had pulled the trigger. Likewise, they had nothing that proved she hadn't.

There had to be something or someone out there who could change that disappointing situation. All they had to do was find it.

"Well, what do you know," Jack announced as Langston turned onto Rolling Hills Drive.

"She's headed to Wallace's house," Anne finished the announcement for him.

"Looks that way."

Sure enough Langston pulled up to the gate in front of the Wallace residence, and the twelve or so feet of iron opened.

Jack parked across the street and far enough back from the house so as not to be easily spotted but with a line of sight to the only way in or out of the property.

"They can't talk on the phone," Anne pointed out with a satisfied smile.

"Not unless they want to risk the records being subpoenaed and the conversation being revealed."

"The best way around leaving evidence of a conversation is to have it face-to-face." Anne folded her arms over her chest. "They're getting their stories straight, I'm sure. Conferring about all the trouble we're causing."

"I agree." Jack considered another thought. "I've also been thinking about Carin's role in all this. Before Neil was murdered," he began, putting the new theory into words for the first time, "it was Eve and Kevin, Mary and Neil. Carin was a sort of fifth wheel. None of the photos you found showed her with a date or a partner. She was always the lone extra."

Anne's brow furrowed as she turned to him. "You're right. She was the extra. The tagalong."

"She was and still is," he went on, "attractive. Apparently smart. What if she was having an affair with Neil or Kevin that whole time and had no desire to have another guy in the mix? She was happy taking whatever she could get from her secret lover."

"If she'd been having an affair with Neil," Anne said, "don't you think that would have come out? It would have been a solid motive for Mary having murdered him. And if Mary had any idea about it, surely she would have mentioned it in the journal."

"Maybe." He let the theory roll around in his head for a bit. "An affair—whichever man was the offending partner—may have been the reason Carin left Crystal Lake in the first place."

"Makes sense," Anne agreed. "Her friends wanted nothing to do with her once they knew." She made a face as if recalling something. "Except Mary mentioned in her journal that she didn't understand why Carin had left. Whatever Eve knew, Mary had no idea."

"Neil could have asked her to leave considering the baby on the way. Carin," Jack offered, "may have felt guilty or abandoned and followed his suggestion."

"But why would she?" Anne countered. "If it was Neil she wanted, why not stay and confront Mary? Why give up so easily?"

Jack smiled. She really had a great mind for investigative work. "That's a very good question. We don't know enough about Carin to make an assessment. But we do know that Eve, on the other hand, was someone Carin probably didn't want to cross. Bearing in mind Kevin's big coup with BioTech and his political aspirations, Eve would likely have sided with Kevin no matter what he'd done. She strikes me as the sort who follows the money. Carin would have known it was a no-win situation."

"Good point." Anne shifted to get more comfortable. "In that scenario, Carin left because Eve found out about the affair. But when the murder happened, she came back to...what? Provide emotional support? Be a cheerleader for Team Eve and Kevin? Make sure she wasn't blamed?"

The realization of what the probable answer was suddenly expanded in Jack's brain. "No, Carin came back to show she was aware of what really happened. By then she was busy sinking her claws into the mega-rich investor Irving Wallace. She was too close to a big payoff to let it go. So she dropped by to leave the message just in case she would need to take advantage of that knowledge in the future."

"And she did. Twenty years later," Anne picked the story up from there, "Irving dropped dead, and poor Carin was left only the paltry sum of five million dollars. The prenup ensured the man's grown children got everything else. So she finds herself back at square one."

"She takes her *paltry* sum and returns to Crystal Lake where her old friends have suddenly risen to fame as Senator and Mrs. Langston. She negotiates a job—one which would not cover the cost of a four-million-dollar home and a six-figure automobile. But with her recent inheritance, she buys the home and the car while the nice salary, and whatever blackmail proceeds flow in keep her afloat in the lifestyle to which she had become accustomed."

Anne smiled. "It's completely logical and fits the pattern. One of the Langstons killed Neil to get him out of the way because he planned to do something or knew something, and they used Mary as the scapegoat. The Langstons got rich from BioTech and launched their dream political career. Carin somehow knew their deep, dark secrets and has milked the couple for all she can get."

Jack held her gaze for a moment. "And your mother spent more than half her life in prison for a crime she didn't commit. She missed raising you…watching you become the amazing young woman you are." He shook his head. "They stole her life."

"They stole my childhood." Anne blinked rapidly, emotion shining in her eyes. "I want to make them pay." Her voice was thick with that emotion.

Jack placed his hand on hers. "We will see to it that happens."

The gate started to open once more. Jack watched as the Langston Mercedes rolled back out.

"I guess leaving a quick message was all she needed to do." This group of friends was definitely up to something.

Anne's breath caught. "Unless she killed her."

Jack met her gaze. Unfortunately, that was a reasonable possibility. Not the most likely one, he figured, but not improbable.

"If she's dead, we can't change that, but we do need to see where Eve goes next. Then we can come back."

"You're right." Anne fastened her seatbelt. "Let's follow her."

They tracked Eve Langston who, surprisingly, returned to her castle-like home without another stop. Then Jack drove back to the Wallace home to follow-up on Carin's status. Anne remained absorbed in her thoughts. He recognized she had a lot to take in with all this…a lot to resolve internally. Her entire adult life she'd ignored thoughts of her biological parents and their tragic history in order to go on with hers. Now she was seeing a different side. All of this had to be overwhelming.

Jack pulled the rental up to the gate and pressed the button for the intercom. He wanted desperately to find answers for her.

"Ms. Wallace is still not available." The woman recognized them from their previous visit. The gate was equipped with a camera as well as an intercom. "If you'll leave your name and number, I will be sure she knows you'd like to speak to her."

Jack leaned forward so that his face was clear for the camera that sat atop the fence. "Jack Brenner from the Colby Agency." He provided his cell number. "Tell her it's important. We know the truth about Neil Reed. She needs to contact me."

"I'll pass along the message."

Jack and Anne exchanged a glance, and then he backed out of the driveway.

"If there had been a fight or any trouble the woman who spoke to you would know it," Anne suggested.

"Which means we don't need to worry about Wallace being wounded and bleeding out on the floor."

"Okay." Anne laughed softly. "I loved your message, by the way. If that doesn't get a response, nothing will."

His cell vibrated on the console. He picked it up and greeted the caller. "Jack Brenner."

"Mr. Brenner," a female voice said, "this is Beatrice Farrell."

He glanced at Anne. "Good afternoon, Ms. Farrell."

"I hope I'm not calling at a bad time."

"Oh, no, ma'am. Your timing is perfect."

Anne was leaning toward him in hopes of hearing the conversation. He wished he had put it on speaker, but that was hard to do while driving.

"I remembered the name of that lab Mary used. It was Trust One. It was the funniest thing. I was watching television, and someone said the word *trust*, and it suddenly came to me. I hope this helps. Please give Anne my best."

Anticipation fired in Jack's veins. "Thank you, Ms. Farrell. This is very helpful."

He ended the call and placed his phone back on the console. "Trust One," he said to Anne who was waiting, staring intently at him. "That's the lab Mary used."

"What are the chances they'll give me a copy of the test?"

"Have your friend Lisa send you a copy of your birth certificate if you have one."

"I do," she said eagerly. "I also have the death certificate that came with the letter from the prison."

"Have her send that too." He drove, his fingers tightening around the steering wheel. "We might be able to get the results since you are Mary's biological daughter. Otherwise, we'll purchase some sort of genetics assessment they offer. She's in their database, so some part of the results of her testing will show up as a match to yours."

"But that takes time, and it might not give us all the information from her original request." Worry tinged Anne's voice.

"Depends on the clerk and what we offer," he suggested. "Maybe we can get everything."

Trust One Lab
Borden Street, 3:00 p.m.

THE PARKING LOT was basically empty. The couple of cars there likely belonged to employees. It was Saturday afternoon. Business had slowed with closing time nearing. Jack removed the five carefully folded one-hundred dollar bills he kept in a hidden slot in his wallet for an emergency just like this one.

"Ready?"

Anne nodded and then got out.

"If there's a chance you could get into trouble for this," she said quietly, "I can do it. I could be just a desperate woman looking for her family. Emotion drives people to do bad things."

He slipped the folded money into his front pocket. "Not necessary. I'm a PI, not a cop. Bending the rules is something I have to do sometimes. The cops don't like it, but they usually don't push it."

She squared her shoulders. "If you're sure."

"Positive." He opened the door, and they entered the waiting area. White walls, industrial-type tile and preformed plastic chairs. The typical sterile environment.

When they reached the counter, a clerk, male, mid-twenties maybe, approached them. He looked beyond ready for his day to be over. It was Saturday, so of course he did. Having someone—a potential customer—walk in the door was not what he wanted at this hour.

"Can I help you?" he said with no enthusiasm.

"Yes." Anne smiled hopefully. "My biological mother had some prenatal paternity testing done here, and I'm hoping to get those results. I have my birth certificate. Her name was—"

"I think," he interrupted, "I'll need a legal order to give you someone else's lab results, even your mother's."

Anne's expression shifted from hopeful to desperate. "I do have my birth certificate and proof she passed away. Are you sure you need anything more?"

He shrugged. "Sorry. There are requests you can make. Or you can do a genetic test and find your matches that way."

Jack placed his hand on the counter, pushed the folded hundreds from beneath his fingers.

"What testing option would you recommend for immediate results?"

The young man stared at the folded bills. He turned to Anne then. "You said you have your birth certificate and maybe a death certificate?"

She nodded. Showed him the images on her phone. "Can I email these to you?"

"Sure thing."

She hit Forward and handed the phone to him. He typed in the email address and pressed Send. Then he gave her a couple of forms.

"Fill these out, and I'll see what I can do."

He went to a desk and worked at his computer while Anne filled out the forms. Jack hoped this would work. A court order could take days or weeks.

Anne laid the pen on the counter. "All done."

"Great." The clerk walked to the printer, picked up some documents, folded them and placed them in an envelope. When he returned to the counter, he handed Anne the envelope, then picked up her forms along with the folded bills. "You'll hear from us as soon as we have results."

He walked back to his desk. Anne glanced at Jack, and he hitched his head toward the door.

They walked out. As soon as they were back in the car he pulled out of the parking slot, and Anne rushed to rip open the envelope.

When he braked to wait for traffic to clear, she pressed her fingers to her lips and turned to him. "It's the report on the paternity test."

He searched her eyes for some sense of the contents of the report. "And?"

"Neil was my father, he's listed as Test Subject #2 and, of course there's mine, Test Subject #1. They used the noninvasive blood test to collect my sample via Mother's blood. Then there's a third set of DNA but no name, just *Test Subject #3*."

"We may not have the name, but we have the guy's DNA. This is good, Anne. Maybe an important piece of the puzzle."

He doubted that Mary Morton would have had the presence of mind to take a sample at the time of her assault. She'd likely sneaked a hair or a toothbrush from Langston's home when she realized she was pregnant and paternity became a concern. Whatever she'd done, it worked.

Before Anne said more his cell vibrated. He picked it up, checked the screen to identify the caller. *Blocked call*. He tapped accept. "Brenner."

"Mr. Brenner, this is Carin Wallace. I think we need to talk."

"I agree." His gaze caught Anne's. "When and where would you like to meet, Ms. Wallace?"

"Why not now? I'll be visiting my old friend

Neil Reed at Crystal Lake Cemetery. See you there."

The sound of the call ending echoed in his ear.

"We got her attention," he told Anne as he pulled out onto the street. "She wants to meet."

"Now?" Her eyes widened. "Where?"

"She'll meet us at the cemetery where your father is buried."

The shock on Anne's face caused a literal pain in his chest.

Damn...he'd gotten way too close to this... to her.

Chapter Seventeen

Crystal Lake
Crystal Lake Cemetery
Ridgefield Road, 3:50 p.m.

Anne stared at the sleek black granite headstone. It was beautiful and at the same time cold and distant. The name *Neil Aaron Reed* was engraved in big letters. Beneath that was *Beloved son*. And of course his dates of birth and death. No mention of his wife or his child.

She hadn't expected to feel anything, but somehow she did. The man buried here was her father. He'd died at a younger age than Anne was right now. No, he hadn't just died—he had been murdered. Not because he'd been a bad man or because he'd done bad things but because someone had wanted what was his.

Fury swelled in her chest. She had never felt so wronged in her life. All those years in foster care could have been avoided. She could have grown up in a good, stable home with good, loving parents...but that opportunity had been stolen from her.

Sure there were plenty of kids in the system who got lucky and ended up with amazing families for their foster care years. But Anne had been one of the unlucky kids who'd bounced from neglectful home to abusive home to overcrowded ones where no one received the care and attention they needed. She supposed it was, in part, because she'd been somewhat difficult between the ages of five and twelve. It was hard when you reached a certain stage in childhood and understood that no one wanted you. Not a single person in the whole world loved you.

And all the stories you had heard about your mother labeled her a monster.

A barrage of those old emotions twisted inside her, had her eyes burning with the need to cry. She would never cry over those years again. Ever. Now she knew things no one had bothered to tell her as a child. According to the journal, this man—her gaze traveled over his name once more—had wanted her. He and Mary had made plans for their future—theirs and their child's. It would have helped so much if she had known this back then. Anne thought of the people closest to her parents. Eve and Kevin Langston. Carin Carter Wallace. Judith Hudson. Beatrice Farrell. Why had no one bothered to find Anne and tell her any of this? Why had they heartlessly allowed her to believe the worst?

Jack rested his hand at the small of her back as if he sensed the turmoil inside her. "You okay?"

She was shaking. She hadn't realized this until he touched her. Her fists were clenched at her sides. *Deep breath*. Reaching for calm, she steadied herself and turned her face up to his. "I will be."

"From what I've learned so far," he offered, "I don't believe your parents were responsible in any way for how this turned out. I also don't think either of them would have wanted you to suffer the hurt and unhappiness you went through as a child. This was a tragedy of someone else's making."

"I'm beginning to see that." She was. For the first time in her life she believed someone had cared and wanted her. The realization that her parents had not thrown her away was so overwhelming it was almost painful. She waffled between wanting to weep and wanting to scream.

The sound of a vehicle arriving drew their attention to the red BMW Alpina that parked behind their rental. Anne recognized the car. Carin Carter Wallace's luxury automobile—the one her dead husband's money had paid for.

Carin emerged from the driver's side, closed the door and strode toward them. The woman was a year younger than Eve. She had managed to maintain her looks considerably better than the other woman. Maybe she'd had more cosmetic surgery or simply better surgeons. Possibly better skin to begin with. Good genes often made all the difference. Additionally, unlike her friend, Carin's wardrobe appeared to be far more stylish and youthful. She could be an influencer on social media.

"Anne Griffin, I presume," Carin announced as she paused a few steps away. Her hands rested on her silk-clad hips. She wore creamy pearl-colored pants and a button-up shirt in the same elegant, flowy fabric that flared open sharply since the top three pearl buttons were unfastened. Her long blond hair and dark sunglasses were emphasized by ruby-red lips. The woman actually looked as if she'd just stepped off the set of a *Vogue* or *Vanity Fair* photo shoot.

Anne gave her a nod.

"Jack Brenner." He thrust out his hand, which prompted Carin to step closer, only the headstone separating them now.

She touched her hand to his briefly. "Carin Wallace."

"Nice of you to join us," Anne said, drawing the woman's attention from Jack.

Carin reached up, removed her designer sunglasses and hung them in the vee of her shirt, which resulted in more showing off of her cleavage. "Have you been here before? Or is this only a drive-by to settle your mother's affairs?"

Anne worked at restraining the anger building inside her. "If by *settle her affairs* you mean find the truth about who murdered my father, yes, that's why I'm here."

Carin laughed softly. "I can't imagine you'll find anything the police didn't." She eyed Jack. "Even with your world-class private investigator." She raised an eyebrow at him. "Your agency has quite the gold-standard reputation…not to mention a fascinating history."

"We do our best." Jack's tone and his expression were proof enough that he was not impressed by the lady.

Anne appreciated that more than he could know. "We've concluded a number of new scenarios since we arrived," she told the woman devouring Jack with her eyes. "You play a major role in most of them."

Her red lips parted in a laugh. "How strange when I wasn't even here during the time frame of the murder."

"You were less than an hour away," Jack countered. "An easy, quick commute."

She looked from him to Anne. "So I'm your prime suspect, am I?"

"One of them," Anne said.

"My money's still on the senator." Jack eased his hands into his pockets and studied Anne for a moment. "I know we talked at length about Carin being at the top of our list, but now that we've met in person—" he gave the older woman a once-over "—I'm not so sure she could have handled the job."

Carin laughed again, but there was no humor in the sound. "It's nice to have someone on my side who recognizes I'm not capable of murder."

Jack was the one chuckling this time. "Oh, I'm confident you're capable. I'm just not sure you could have pulled it off without getting caught. The person who murdered Neil Reed was very careful. Meticulous, even. Unless the police were completely incompetent, the killer left no evidence whatsoever."

Anne nodded. She got where he was going now. "A mastermind." She made a *no way* face at Carin. "You're right. She's obviously not the one."

"Whatever you believe," the older woman snapped, "your mother is the *one* who murdered Neil. She was jealous and vindictive. She despised her life. I remember her fantasizing about having a life just like the one Eve had planned. I guess she thought if she got Neil out of the way—"

"She could have Kevin," Anne interrupted. "I can't deny that scenario is a possibility. Not since we found the lab she used." This idea had only just occurred to Anne. She hoped Jack would approve.

Confusion flashed on Carin's unlined face before she could restrain it. "I'm not following. What lab?"

"The one she used for a prenatal DNA test to determine whether Neil was my father or if it was..." She stared directly into the other woman's eyes. "Kevin."

The impact of the words visibly shook Carin Carter Wallace.

Anne kept going, determined not to let up now. "Her journal was very insightful. I'm just sorry she didn't allow me to see it before she died. It would have changed everything for her... for me too."

"I hate to be the one to tell you this," Carin said, the shock under control now, "but Mary Morton was a liar. A consummate liar and a cheater. She betrayed Neil. She betrayed all of us."

"Kevin didn't seem to mind," Anne countered. She glanced at Jack then. "I think you're right. It probably was Kevin who murdered him. He stole Neil's offer from BioTech, assaulted his wife and got away with it all."

"Until now," Jack pointed out.

"I would watch myself where the senator is concerned," Carin advised. "He'll react strongly to such unfounded allegations."

"What will he do?" Anne demanded, taking a step in the other woman's direction. "Kill me too? He's already started a fire at the hotel where we were staying. He has his thugs following us."

Carin's eyes narrowed to slits. "You never know what a cornered animal will do next."

Anne smiled. "Good point because he is an animal. My mother isn't the only woman he assaulted. But I'm guessing you knew that already."

"Knowledge is power in the world of politics," Jack noted.

Carin backed up a step. "I warn you—" she looked from one to the other "—do not go down this path. You will regret it."

"A lot of people are going to have regrets when we're done," Anne tossed right back at her. "But it won't be us. Believe that if you believe nothing else."

"If only you had proof," Carin bemoaned, then she laughed.

"You mean," Anne suggested, "like the DNA of the person my mother feared might be my father after he assaulted her? I have the lab report. It's all there."

Red lips pursed in fury, Carin did an about-face and marched back to her extravagant automobile.

When she'd driven away, Jack turned to Anne

and clapped his hands. "Very good. I doubt she's been that rattled in decades."

"Probably around three." Anger stirred inside Anne. "I hope she rushes back to the Langstons and tells them every word we said."

"We're really going to have to watch our backs now," he cautioned.

"If we shake them up enough, one of them is bound to get fired up and make a mistake."

"That's the part that worries me," Jack confessed. "Like the woman said, when an animal gets cornered, you never know what it might do."

Anne met his gaze once more. "I'm not afraid. Not with you on my side."

He took her hand in his and gave it a squeeze. "No fear, but we will proceed with extreme caution."

Anne nodded, then looked at the headstone once more. A small flower arrangement had been tucked against it. The blooms had drooped and fallen free, and the leaves had withered and turned brown. She couldn't help wondering who had brought the flowers. Mr. Reed, perhaps?

She crouched down and looked for a card. No card. The small bundle fell over, revealing something beneath it. The bronze color almost caused her to miss the roundish object. Anne tapped it and realized it was some sort of metal. She pulled it free of the dirt. Someone had partially buried it next to the headstone. There was an inscription.

Mary Morton.

Anne's breath caught. Beneath the name was her date of birth and death as well as *Cremation Services of Crystal Lake*. It was one of those mini urns...part of her mother's ashes. But who put them here?

She pushed to her feet and showed the urn to Jack. "Someone brought her here."

Anne had been told Mary was cremated, but she never asked what became of her remains. She hadn't cared at the time.

But she cared now. Maybe her mother had one friend left in this town after all.

Jack pulled out his cell and tapped in a search. "They're still open." He looked to Anne. "We can see if they'll tell us who picked up her ashes."

"Let's do it."

Jack helped her to tuck the small urn next to the headstone and cover it properly. Anne dusted her hands off. At least her parents were together now.

Cremation Services
North Virginia Street, 5:30 p.m.

THE RATHER SMALL brick building was nothing like a funeral home. There were no rooms for services related to viewings and funerals. This was a place where cremations were performed and a lobby where the ashes were picked up for whatever the family intended. Somewhere beyond the lobby was likely the business office.

"Hello," the man behind the counter said, a faint smile on his lips. "May I help you?"

Anne worked up a smile in return. "I'm here to ask about my mother, Mary Morton. She died at Logan Correctional Center."

The man slowly nodded. "Yes, I'm familiar. I was contacted by a friend who contracted our services. We picked up Ms. Morton and fulfilled the service requested."

"Who contracted the service? I want to thank them for taking care of her arrangements since I was unreachable. I had no idea she'd died until days later."

When the man hesitated, Jack withdrew a business card and placed it on the counter. "We want to keep this as discreet as possible. No need to involve the authorities or warrants."

The man studied the card. "Judith Hudson. She took care of everything."

"Thank you," Jack said.

Anne managed a nod of thanks before Jack ushered her outside. Why would Judith not have mentioned having taken care of the arrangements? Why be so secretive?

Frustration rolled through Anne. If she'd only

been trying to help, why act as if she'd committed some crime?

Maybe the need to do this final act for Mary had been about guilt instead of friendship.

Chapter Eighteen

Judith's Cocktail Lounge
Williams Street, 7:15 p.m.

"You should eat." Jack nodded toward the plate the waiter had placed in front of Anne a good fifteen minutes ago.

She stared at the delicious-smelling orange-marinated chicken in the bed of fluffy rice. She just didn't feel the urge to eat no matter that it looked and smelled so good. "You're right." She picked up her fork and poked at the rice.

He'd started devouring the ramen he'd ordered the moment it arrived. Like her entrée, it looked great. And smelled just as good—garlicky and gingery.

But her taste buds just wouldn't rise to the occasion. She kept thinking of how her parents were finally together again after all these years. And how she had lost so much—they had lost so much—because someone decided that what they wanted was more important. It just wasn't fair.

They had asked to see Judith as soon as they arrived. She was here but busy. The waitress promised the owner would pop over to their table as soon as she could. That had been half an hour ago.

Anne poked a forkful of rice flavored with orange sauce into her mouth and forced herself to chew. There was a lot in this life—in this world—that wasn't fair. People went to prison every day for crimes they didn't commit. Were harmed in some way when they had done nothing to deserve such treatment. She understood this, but somehow seeing an up-close look at the life her parents had lived and all the potential they had lost made her want to cry.

She squeezed her eyes shut. *Not going to cry. Not now.*

"Hey." Jack's hand rested atop hers.

She opened her eyes and met his gaze. The concern and kindness there caused hope to bloom deep inside her.

"Sometimes these things get really tough before they get better," he assured her, "but we're on the downhill side of this. We know what and who we're looking at. It's going to get better from here."

Although they were in a public place, the tables were spaced far enough apart and the music playing in the background allowed a sense of privacy. She appreciated that and his words more than she could say.

She poked at a piece of chicken. "Thanks. I really would not have gotten through this without you." When she popped it into her mouth and chewed she almost moaned. The chicken was amazing. So tender, and the spice level was the perfect balance of sweet and zesty.

He grinned. "If yours is half as good as mine…" He made a satisfied sound.

"It's great." Her appetite was at full attention now. "You were right."

"Good." He ate for a moment more. "You mentioned that you wouldn't have gotten through this without me." He shrugged. "If you recall, you wouldn't be in the middle of this if I hadn't knocked on your door."

This was true.

"You recognized something I didn't want to see," she countered. "I wanted to go on with my life without looking back." She shrugged. "Without believing that the past mattered. I was wrong, and you helped me see that. In my case anyway, I had to come back and see this through. Otherwise, sometime down the line I would have regretted not finishing this." She looked out the window for a moment. Watched the Saturday-evening traffic roll past. "Maybe when I had children of my own it would have hit me particularly hard. But the past—the story I didn't want to hear—would still have been haunting me. This was the right thing to do, and I'm so glad you helped me see that."

"I'm glad I've been able to help."

She suddenly felt a little embarrassed. "I'm sorry. I know you've only been doing your job, but it has felt like more to me." Might as well get that out there on the table. Particularly after last night.

His smile warmed her chest. "If I may be totally honest, this hasn't felt like work since I read Mary's journal. We're basically strangers, but I hope we can change that going forward."

After last night, she had been having that same thought—the same hope. It was such a relief to hear that she wasn't alone in those feelings. "I would like that very much."

"I'm so sorry to keep you waiting." Judith appeared at their table. She grabbed a nearby chair no one was using and settled in. "I'm hearing all sorts of gossip about what you two have been up to." She looked from Anne to Jack and then to their half-finished food. "I hope our amazing chef hasn't disappointed you."

"The food is great." Anne reached for her cocktail. Same one as she made at home—lemonade with strawberries and vodka. "And so is the cocktail."

"Both are excellent," Jack agreed. "But... I would be interested in the gossip you're hearing."

Judith waved off the comment. "Nothing fascinating, really." She smiled. "Other than how riled up the whole tribe is."

Anne savored the lemony vodka as she sat her glass down. "Carin and Eve aren't too happy with us. The senator either, I suspect."

"I'm sure you heard," Jack interjected, "about the Water's Edge Hotel—those were our rooms. An odd sort of coincidence, wouldn't you say?"

"Indeed," Judith agreed. "I was so glad to hear the two of you were out when that happened. Sounds exactly like one of those scare tactics they use in the movies. Hard to believe it happened right here in our little town."

"Not really," Anne argued. "It's all tied to the murder of Neil Reed. I think we both know the wrong person went to prison for that heinous crime."

The older woman's eyebrows reared up her forehead. "Some would agree with you. Others probably not."

Anne patted her lips with her linen napkin and decided to cut to the chase. "Why did you arrange for her body to be cremated?"

Judith stared back at Anne with the same firm look in her eyes. "Who else was going to do it?

Would you have preferred the state did away with her? You know, they donate unclaimed bodies for research. Is that what you would have preferred?"

Anne flinched. Until a few days ago she would have preferred exactly that. To have one's body donated for medical research was a good thing. But now she wasn't sure she could say that about Mary's body. The woman had been her mother... and she had suffered more than her share of neglect and abandonment in her life.

"No," Anne admitted. "Thank you for taking care of her."

Judith blinked once, twice, three times as if having difficulty holding back the emotion shining in her eyes. "It was the least I could do."

"And thank you for seeing that some of her ashes were buried next to his headstone. I'm sure she would have appreciated that."

"It felt like the right thing to do."

"I do have one question though." Anne understood that whatever moment they'd just shared would be shattered by this single query.

Judith lifted her chin as if bracing for the unexpected. "What is that?"

"Why didn't you or any of her other friends see that I was placed in a good home? I know what you said before, but I want the truth this time."

It was a simple question, really. Mary had so-called friends. Neil had a father. And yet no one bothered to do a single thing for the child born to the two.

Anne had stopped resenting the friends and family who should have stepped in. What was done was done. But how had they lived with themselves? This was the part she would never understand.

Judith stared at the table for a moment, unable to meet Anne's eyes. "It was a difficult time for many. Neil was dead, and his father suddenly lost his wife. The man was beside himself with grief. I think he saw you—" she finally met Anne's gaze "—as an extension of your mother and, therefore, unworthy of his attention or support. It was wrong, obviously. But you can't tell a man anything when he's that wounded. I'm sure at some point he realized his mistake, but it was too late by then."

"And what about you? Carin? Eve? All of you claimed to be Mary's friends until near the end."

"I can't speak for Carin or for Eve," Judith admitted. "But I will say that something happened between those three. I have no idea what it was, but things changed. Your mother was suddenly on the outside. I tried to talk to her to find out what was going on, but she wouldn't talk to me. She avoided me and everyone else."

Anne stared at her, waiting for the rest.

The older woman closed her eyes and drew in a heavy breath. When she opened her eyes once more they were liquid with emotion. "Jerry had found someone new and younger. A woman already pregnant with his child—something I could never give him. I was in a bad place. A place I couldn't find my way back from for a very long time. By the time I realized I should have helped you, you were in the system, and no one was giving me any information. I wasn't family and my efforts were futile. I even went to Preston, your grandfather, and asked for his help, but he was still in that awful place where he hated everyone—especially you simply because you were alive and his son wasn't."

Anne wanted to resent this woman for her failure. She wanted to be angry with her for letting Mary and her down. But Judith was only human, and she'd gotten through that time period the only way she could. What happened was not her fault.

"Judith." Jack drew her attention to him. "I fully understand your reasons, as I'm sure Anne does." He looked to her, and she nodded. "But if you recall anything at all that might help us find the truth about who murdered Neil, you could help Anne now. She needs this to be settled. She deserves that, as does her mother. Help us."

Anne battled the tears stinging her eyes. She held her breath, dared to hope.

Judith placed both palms against the table as if she might push herself up out of her chair and walk away. She stared at that space where her hands rested, not meeting either of their gazes.

Finally, she looked up, this time at Jack. "There was serious trouble brewing." Her voice was low. "Neil and Kevin came to blows at dinner is the way I heard it. They were at the new house Kevin was planning to buy. They'd done one of those *trying it out for a night* deals. He and Eve were getting married in October, and they wanted to get settled before the wedding and honeymoon."

"Do you know what the fight was about?" Jack asked.

"It was…" She looked to Anne. "About the baby—you. Bear in mind that I heard all this thirdhand. Eve had told Carin and Carin told me."

"Kevin took advantage of my mother." Fury built inside Anne.

Judith nodded. "He claimed it was a one-time moment of weakness that Mary instigated, but I didn't believe it. Frankly, anyone who really knew him wouldn't have believed it. But Eve had her reasons for taking his word. She wanted to marry the man who would be a senator one day. A man who had taken a position from the *Steve Jobs* of research laboratory developers. Eve knew Kevin was moving up, and she intended to rise with him."

Anne struggled to keep her anger at bay. "Carin knew too. That's why she left."

"I can't say for sure," Judith confessed, "but she knew it was all going to hit the fan, and she wanted no part of it."

"Do you," Jack asked, "believe Kevin Langston killed Neil?"

Judith held his gaze for a long, heart pounding moment. "No."

No? Before Anne could demand an explanation, the woman went on.

"I believe Eve did it for him. Kevin would never have dared do anything that might damage his reputation. No way." She shrugged. "Although he had trouble keeping his trousers fastened, he, evidently, believed that particular sin was forgivable given the number of powerful men who've gotten away with it. But he was far too self-absorbed to consider risking it all by committing murder."

"Why," Anne demanded, "did you never tell anyone?"

Again, the older woman hesitated before answering. "I was afraid."

Anne shook her head, swung her gaze to the

window to prevent the other woman from seeing the accusation there. How could a woman who operated her own successful business be afraid?

"I did try."

"How so, Judith?" Jack asked.

Anne turned back to the conversation. She certainly wanted to hear this one.

"I went to the detective—Detective Jones. Not at his office. I was too afraid. I went to his house. He and his wife had two kids, and they were living in a dump. I think he was embarrassed that I showed up there, but his financial status was irrelevant to me."

"You told him," Jack pressed, "about your suspicions."

Judith moved her head up and down with a solemnness that finished the story before she said another word. "We sat on his back porch. I remember the house badly needed painting, and it was hot that evening. Just unusually miserable. But he heard me out and wrote everything down. He said he would let me know if he had any more questions."

Anne knew exactly what happened. "He never had any more questions."

"No. I, on the other hand, was suddenly in the battle of my life with my husband and with the state licensing board. It took me nearly a year to get all the local government offices related to running a business like mine off my back. I suppose I was lucky I wasn't murdered."

"You were lucky," Jack confirmed.

Anne thought of the house they had visited where Harlan Jones lived. It was certainly not the same one Judith spoke about. The high-end SUV and fishing boat weren't exactly cheap either.

"I noticed," Judith went on, "later, maybe around Christmas, that the detective had moved up in the world. He bought a really nice house, moved his family there." She laughed, a soft, bitter sound. "I suspect he quickly recognized which side his bread was buttered on."

"Did Carin or Eve or her husband ever approach you about what you told the detective?" Jack asked.

"No. Carin had moved away and was doing her own kind of fishing for a rich husband. Eve and Kevin moved to Chicago to be nearer his new job. They only returned to Crystal Lake after he was elected to the US Senate. Ten years ago, I think. They built that enormous house and have been showing off ever since."

"But they all remain friendly with you," Anne said. "I'm guessing you put the word out about us after we talked that first time."

"They pretend to be my friends," Judith clarified. "But we don't socialize unless they come here. As for passing the word along, I apologize, but it gave me great pleasure. I simply couldn't help myself." She frowned suddenly. "Dear Lord, I hope it wasn't my fault that the hotel was set on fire."

Jack waved off the idea. "They would have found out from someone."

This didn't appear to assuage her guilt. "I really am sorry if I contributed to that in any way."

"We should go." Anne finished off her cocktail. "We've had a long day." She set her gaze on the older woman's. "Thank you again for what you did for my mother. I should have been the one, but I was not in the right place for that."

"I was glad I could." Judith smiled. "For the record, I wish I had done the right thing for you as well. I've regretted that for all these years." She stood. "Tonight is on the house." She nodded to Jack. "Thank you for bringing her here."

"Yes, ma'am."

Anne floated between elation and anger on the drive back to their motel. It wasn't that anything Judith had told her helped prove who Neil's killer was—not in a strong enough or solid enough way to have the case reopened. But all of it made Anne feel a good deal better.

"Tomorrow," Jack said, "we'll pay another visit to the detective. The things Judith revealed will give us some leverage."

"I can't see Jones admitting to anything at this stage in his life," she countered. "Not unless it involved some deal where he got immunity. Or maybe," she added with a laugh, "he wants rid of his wife."

"Depending on which side of the political fence the DA in this county is on, it's possible he or she might be willing to go that route—a deal, I mean—if it brought down a dirty senator."

Anne chewed her lip. "Carin probably knows all the gritty details. But I'm guessing she won't change sides for any reason."

"Not unless—" Jack glanced at Anne "—she's the one who took care of the situation. Just because she had moved away doesn't mean she didn't come back for a few hours or a day."

"I'm still leaning toward Eve. She had the most to lose—besides the senator, I mean. Judith might be right about him. He may not have had the guts to do the job." Anne stared out at the darkening sky. The sun was setting. It would be full-on dark soon. "Then again, maybe he hired someone."

"Possibly. But the more people involved in a secret, the less likely it is to stay secret. If Eve or Carin were willing, that would have been the safest route for the future."

"Unless there was something else," Anne said

slowly, sharing her thoughts as they occurred, "that motivated her. I can't wrap my head around the idea that Carin would take a man's life for a friend. It just seems like something that requires a more personal motive. Unless you're nothing more than a cold-blooded killer."

"Or desperate," Jack offered.

"But again, what was her motive? What was she desperate about? Kevin Langston wasn't her husband-to-be. Why kill someone over a betrayal that had no impact on her? She was working on Irving Wallace by then. She had the most to gain by sticking with Wallace."

"Ah." Jack glanced in Anne's direction. "We can't be certain there was no impact to her. If the senator was a cheater, maybe Carin was one of his lovers. She may have believed he intended to drop Eve for her. With Wallace there was that little problem of the prenup, and she had no leverage to prevent it."

"I should have thought of that one." Anne frowned. "Perhaps Carin was friendlier with Kevin than she ever was with Eve."

"When Eve found out," Jack went on, "she was grateful Carin had taken care of one problem, just not grateful enough to share her future husband."

"Until they had no choice." Anne considered the timeline. "Once Carin's rich husband died—

leaving her near penniless, in her mind—she decided to come back and call in the marker."

Jack slowed for the turn into the motel. As he shifted into Park, he pulled out his cell. He stared at the screen. "Speak of the devil." He showed a text to Anne.

It's Carin. Meet me at the house on Fairlawn. We need to talk. Can't do it on the phone.

"What if it's not really her?" Worry edged into Anne's thoughts.

"We can counter with a different meeting place."

She shook her head. "We shouldn't take the risk. If she's willing to talk, we should do this her way. She might change her mind."

"We'll take necessary precautions," he assured her as he backed out and pulled back onto the road. "We won't just walk in the door."

Anne wasn't worried. She trusted Jack completely.

Chapter Nineteen

Journal Entry
Thirty Years Ago
October 1

Neil died on the Saturday before Labor Day.

I cried nearly every waking hour for days. I didn't know how I could go on.

Somehow they had decided to fast-track the trial, and it would begin in a few weeks. I asked my court-appointed attorney to get word to Neil's father that I was innocent. But he either did not or Mr. Reed didn't believe me. I was sure he was devastated too. Especially after Mrs. Reed's heart attack. It was all completely unbelievable.

My world had fallen to pieces.

Neil was gone.

I couldn't imagine that anyone really believed I murdered him…but they did. I sat in that jail cell—without bond—because they believed it.

The detective, even my own attorney, looked at me as if I was evil.

I spent most of my time with both arms wrapped around my belly and you and wondered what on earth would become of you. I realized that if the trial began as scheduled, I would be in prison months before you were born. I was so scared for you. Neil's father wouldn't talk to me, so how could I convince him to take care of you?

The weeks passed and the trial commenced and no one believed me. They didn't even hear me. They merely looked at me and saw evil.

A social worker came to see me to discuss my signing over rights to you, but I refused. How could I willingly do that? I so hoped if I waited things would turn around. I would not lose you unless I had no other choice. You are my child— my only remaining part of Neil. You have my word that I tried everything possible to take care of you—to be your mother.

When the worst happened, I prayed that Mr. Reed would come through. I was sure he hated me. Who wouldn't under the circumstances? If he believed I killed his son—his only child— how could he feel anything else? But he shouldn't hate you. You were as much Neil's as mine.

I remember telling Neil that after you were born his father would likely be more involved in our lives, but he didn't think so. He said his father had always kept him at arm's length. I can't say that I found him particularly nice to me. I always assumed he thought I wasn't good enough for his only son. Perhaps he was simply busy with all his real estate holdings. Whatever the case, I was alone.

I had never felt so helpless in my life.

But I had to be strong. I had to somehow make them see that I would never have hurt Neil. I loved him with every part of my being.

All these years later, you, of course, know what happened. I wish I could give you the answer to why it happened the way it did and the identity of who hurt your father...but I honestly don't know. I only know that I came home and found him shot and dying. He tried to talk but no words came, and then he was gone.

I am sure he would have told me how much he loved both of us if he had been able to say the words. But those words weren't necessary. I knew without a doubt how much he loved me, just as I loved him. Still do. And we both desperately loved you. Still do.

I am sorrier than you will ever know that you came into this world with so much against you already. That is my biggest regret.

Be strong and always know that you were wanted and loved deeply.

And if somehow this journal helps you find

the truth, I am glad for you. I have no regrets about the choices I have made. If I could start over, I would follow the same path to the man I loved with all my heart.

Be safe, dear daughter. I have always loved you.

Chapter Twenty

Johnsburg
Fairlawn Drive, 10:00 p.m.

The house was dark.

Jack saw no other vehicles. He eased to the side of the street opposite the house Mary and Neil had shared.

He shut off the engine, and the headlights went out.

"I don't see her snazzy red car."

"I didn't see any vehicles parked along the street." Jack reviewed the slow roll along Fairlawn they had just made. "The only two houses on the street that appear to be occupied have one vehicle each in the drives, but nothing Carin would be caught operating."

Anne released her seat belt and turned around to try and scan the street, but with only one streetlamp at the end of the block there was little to see.

"Should we go in first?" She turned back to him.

Jack had an uneasy feeling about this. He reached across the console and opened the glove box. The feel of her breath on his neck had him turning to face her. "We could always go back to our motel and insist on doing this in the daylight."

She smiled. He didn't have to see—he felt it. "There are things I would much prefer to do tonight, but maybe this will give us the rest of what we need to finish this."

"Okay." He brushed his lips across hers. Then he took the handgun and flashlight from the glove box. He didn't like carrying a handgun when digging around in a cold case. It generally wasn't necessary. But he never went on assignment without one. Tonight his instincts were on fire.

"I have the key." She dug it from her bag and held it up for him to see.

"Okay." He turned off the interior lights and reached for his door. "Stay put until I come around to your door."

The air was hot and thick with humidity as he exited the car, closing the door softly. He scanned the street. Spotted no movement, although he couldn't be certain as dark as it was. Keeping his steps as quiet as possible, he walked around to the passenger-side door and opened it. He kept watch while Anne climbed out.

They hurried across the narrow street and into the overgrown yard that fronted the abandoned house. It still struck him as odd that Mary's and Neil's things—at least some of them—remained in the house. From the looks of this part of the street there wasn't that much going on in the way of gentrification. Still, nearly thirty years was a long time for a house to sit abandoned. Why had Preston Reed kept it all this time like some sort of shrine? Actually, that was probably the answer.

As with their last visit, they made their way onto the porch, thankfully without turning on the flashlight. Anne used the light from the screen of her cell, which was far dimmer than the flashlight app, to find the door key. If anyone was watching them, Jack would prefer that they stay as invisible as possible.

The door opened before the key was even in the lock. She stared up at him, and he leaned close and whispered, "Stay behind me."

She nodded her understanding, her temple brushing against his jaw.

For several seconds he stood just beyond the doorway and listened for any sound and allowed his senses to sharpen in the darkness. When he was satisfied, he moved forward. Anne stuck close behind him. He closed the door, gritting his teeth as the click echoed in the silence.

They moved through the house, checking room after room and finding nothing beyond what had been there the first time they walked through the house.

"What was the point of this?" Anne murmured.

"Maybe she was delayed," Jack offered, keeping his voice low as well.

"Maybe." Anne walked to the back door. She held her cell up to look at the door with the light from the screen. "I don't remember the door being boarded shut."

Jack turned on the flashlight and joined her at the back door. The glass area in the upper part of the door was now covered with boards. He reached for the knob, gave it a twist, and though it turned freely the door didn't budge.

"Maybe someone saw us over here on Wednesday and Reed sent a caretaker over to secure the place."

"But they left the front door unlocked?" Anne countered. "And if there's a caretaker, why let the place grow up like this?"

Very good questions. "Let's go," he said sharply, a new kind of worry kicking him in the gut.

Before they were out of the kitchen the smell of gasoline reached his nostrils. The odor was immediately followed by a whoosh he recognized all too well.

The front door was engulfed in flames. He hurried to the nearest window. Anne rushed to yet another.

The sashes wouldn't budge. Obviously they'd been screwed or nailed shut. Or years and layers of paint had sealed them shut.

"This way," he called out.

They hurried from room to room, checked all the windows. All were secured in the closed position.

By the time they were back in the kitchen, flames were climbing up the side of the house, dancing over the windows. Smoke had started to fill the air.

Urgency fired in Jack's gut. He grabbed Anne by the hand and rushed back to the bedroom Mary had used as an office. He grabbed the chair.

"Stand back and call 911." As soon as she moved away, he crashed the window with the chair. He used the chair to shove the remaining jagged pieces of glass from the frame, then he tossed it aside and used his hands to finish busting out the wood parts. The flames were climbing that side of the house too. They only had moments before it would be too late. This old house was going up in flames like dry kindling.

"Help is on the way," she said as he pulled her toward him.

"We can't wait."

As if on cue she started to cough.

They had to get out now.

"I'm going to pick you up and set your feet on the windowsill, and then you need to jump as far forward as possible." The idea that they had no idea what was in all that overgrown grass and shrubs outside—benches, flowerpots, yard ornaments—twisted his gut. Part of him wanted to go first and check out the situation. But the smoke filling his lungs warned there was no time. He had to get Anne out of here.

She hesitated. "You'll be right behind me?"

"I'll be right behind you."

"Okay."

He put his hands on her waist and lifted her upward. She planted her feet on the windowsill and leaned forward.

"Go!" he shouted as he released her.

She jumped, landing in the dense shrubs beyond the flames.

Jack went next. He grabbed onto the sides of the window frame, the heat scorching his fingers, and lunged into the air.

He plowed into the thick brush and shrubs. His knee contacted something hard.

He clenched his jaw against the pain and scrambled to his feet. He grabbed Anne by the arm and started through the junglelike landscape. Pain roared up his leg and his knee refused to work properly, but he managed to hobble quickly forward.

He checked the rental car, then they climbed inside. His body shuddered with the effort of working through the pain.

Anne stared out the car window at the house that was now fully engulfed. Thankfully there were no inhabited properties on either side of it.

They would need to make a statement when the police arrived.

Anne turned to him. "I want to go to her house."

Jack wasn't sure that was a good idea. "We should wait for the police."

"No," she argued. "I want to see Carin Wallace's face and find out why the hell she did this if she wasn't the one to kill my father. If we wait she could be long gone."

Jack started the car and pulled onto the street. By the time they arrived at the intersection at the end of the block, firetrucks were roaring toward them, lights and sirens blaring.

Knowing that help was on-site made leaving more palatable. They drove the few miles to Barrington and the extravagant residence of Carin Carter Wallace. She likely wouldn't answer and surely wouldn't open the gate.

To Jack's surprise, the gate was open.

He rolled forward, going slowly. He scanned

the landscape as best he could, following the path of the headlights as they drew closer to the house.

"Her car is here." Anne pointed to the red vehicle.

There was an SUV also. Range Rover. White. Didn't look familiar.

Jack parked. "We should approach the house with caution. We can't be sure who's in there with her and what's happened."

Anne nodded. "Got it. I'll follow your lead."

They emerged from the rental and walked toward the front door. Lights were on inside, suggesting someone was there. Only two steps separated the stone parking area from the double door entry. One of the doors was ajar.

Jack hesitated. He drew his weapon. "You should call 911 again and give them this address. Whatever has happened here, it isn't likely to be good."

Anne made the call, staying close behind him as he entered the house. He didn't have to go far before he spotted the first sign of trouble.

A suitcase on the floor by the table where a car fob lay in a glass catchall.

"In here."

The voice, male, was one Jack recognized. He moved toward the entrance to a great room, where Preston Reed sat on the sofa. A few feet away Carin Wallace lay on the floor, blood pooled around her middle.

Anne gasped, and though Jack wanted to rush to the wounded woman's side to check her vitals, he held his position in front of Anne. He had to protect her at all costs. He surveyed the man seated on the sofa. "Do you have a gun, Mr. Reed?"

He nodded, gestured to the floor.

Jack walked closer, saw the handgun on the floor. He kicked it away, sending it under the coffee table. With the immediate threat out of the way, he checked Carin Carter Wallace for a pulse. Considering her eyes were open, pupil's fixed and dilated, and her chest wasn't moving, he didn't hold out much hope that she was still alive. Her skin was cool, no pulse at the base of her throat. He shook his head at Anne, who stood a few feet away, staring in shock.

Jack stood and approached the man on the couch. "What happened, Mr. Reed?"

"Your visit—" he looked beyond Jack to Anne "—got me to thinking. The more I thought about all that you said, the more I questioned what I thought I had always known. About seven I went to the senator's house and demanded answers. He wasn't there, of course. Or if he was he was hiding." He shook his head, his face and posture weary. "So I guess I took out my emotions on his wife. I grilled her. Even shook her. She'll probably charge me with assault, but I didn't hit her."

Anne moved closer. "What did she say?"

"She said it was Carin. That Carin was the one who killed my son. She'd been having an affair with him, and when he refused to leave Mary, she disappeared." He exhaled a big breath. "Except then she came back to try one last time. But Neil wouldn't change his mind." Preston's gaze settled on Anne's. "He loved your mother too much. He wasn't giving up her and you for anything or anyone." His jaw tightened. "He always was hardheaded, just like his mother."

Jack and Anne shared a look.

"Then you came here?" Jack suggested.

The older man nodded. "She had a gun, but I took it away from her. She was in a big rush to get out of here. We argued and I tried to force her to tell me the truth, but she just kept laughing at me. She repeated two or three times that it would all be over after tonight." He shook his head. "But I didn't understand. Then we struggled and the gun went off."

He glanced at the woman on the floor. "She killed my son."

Anne's hands went to her face.

Jack considered the man again. "Did she admit this to you, Mr. Reed?"

"She did." He nodded. "She laughed when she

said it. She said it was time I knew the truth but it was too bad no one else ever would." His gaze dropped to the floor. "I had to stop her...to see that she paid for what she had done."

Sirens blaring outside drew their attention to the windows.

"The police are here now." Jack slid his arm around Anne's waist and pulled her closer to him. "You can tell them what you just told us, and they'll figure it out."

Reed pushed to his feet as if he were eager to do so. "I'm ready." He stared at Anne. "I'm sorry I didn't believe Mary."

While he continued to speak to Anne, Jack studied him closer. Something about this didn't feel right. Then he spotted the oily-looking stain on his shirt around the left shoulder area. For such a warm night he was wearing a long-sleeved shirt, and the right sleeve was torn.

"Mr. Reed—" Jack ushered Anne behind him "—I'm sure this has all been a shock. Did Carin also tell you about the fire at the Fairlawn house?"

Reed's gaze swung to Jack. "What? What fire?"

Jack was close enough to smell the odor of gasoline clinging to his clothes. And the faintest scent of smoke.

Anne suddenly stepped around Jack. "It was you. I smell the gasoline. You tried to kill us."

Reed dove for the gun.

Jack was on top of him before his fingers could wrap around the grip. Anne snatched up the gun and tossed it across the room.

"It was all her fault," he railed, his face twisted with fury as he tried to glare up at Anne. "Mary didn't want him to take the job with BioTech. It was too risky, she claimed, so he turned down the offer. I tried to change his mind. We were set to make a fortune. I'd invested heavily when he told me about Smith and his offer, and I needed him on the inside so he could feed me information. But he refused." He turned his gaze to the floor as if the rest was too awful or too humiliating to say with anyone staring at him. "He refused," he repeated, the words muffled by the rug beneath his face. "He was my son, and he refused. He chose her over me."

"What happened?"

Preston looked at Jack. "I always carried a handgun. It had belonged to my father. Being in real estate, he'd warned me to carry it when I was just a young man. And he was right. I learned the hard way how dangerous some people who didn't want to be evicted could be." He shifted into a sitting position. Exhaled a heavy breath. "All those rental properties. I was in debt over my head. I don't know what happened. Neil and I were arguing, and suddenly I had the gun in my hand. I killed him. I didn't mean to... I only wanted to make him see what my life was like. I had protected him from that ugliness." He shook his head. "It was an accident. I tried to make him listen, and it went off." He started to sob. "I killed him. I killed him."

The police poured into the house. Jack lowered his weapon to the floor and nudged it away with his foot.

Anne stood next to him and cried softly while they cuffed her grandfather.

She finally knew the truth. Her mother hadn't killed her father.

Barrington Police Department
Northwest Highway
Sunday, July 13, 5:00 a.m.

ANNE HAD NEVER been so tired in her life.

Preston Reed had officially confessed to the murder of his son as well as Carin Carter Wallace. Much of what he had told her and Jack at the Wallace home had been lies. At that point he had been trying to frame Carin for the murder. But it was him. Carin never had an affair with Neil. Preston Reed had not gone to the Langston home and confronted Eve as he claimed. He'd come up with this desperate plan to use Carin in order to lure Anne and Jack to the Fairlawn house.

None of this horrific mystery had turned out the way Anne had expected.

Senator and Eve Langston were not guilty of participating in any way in the murder of Neil Reed. The senator was only guilty of being a bad friend and trying to steal the job Neil had decided he didn't want anyway. Carin, on the other hand, had known about the senator's predilection for young interns. After her husband's death, she had returned to Crystal Lake determined to glom onto the Langstons since they were rich and powerful by that point. She had enough blackmail material based on Kevin's proclivity to cheat on his wife. It had been time, in her opinion, to cash in.

All the people who should have been there for Mary and Neil had let them down for their own selfish reasons. Eve and Kevin because they hadn't wanted to get involved and have any sort of connection to murder on the record. Judith and Carin were guilty of the same. Each had her own problems and selfishly turned their backs on Mary when she needed them most. Even Ms. Farrell had, on some level, kept her head down to avoid the fallout. No one had really tried.

No matter that Anne had never allowed herself to care about her mother, she was glad that she was able to clear her name. To do what no one else had been willing to try. The memories would be with Anne for the rest of her life—the good and the bad. She was immensely thankful to the Colby Agency—to Jack—for helping her uncover and sort out those real memories.

"We're free to go," Jack announced as he walked into the tiny office.

The chief of police had given his office to Anne for some privacy. She stood, pushed all the painful thoughts out of her mind. It was time to move on. Time to tuck away all these memories of the past and murder and look to the future. Her parents would want her to be happy. And Jack had been right—they would be proud of how far she had come despite the bumpy start she had gotten in life.

Jack smiled at her, made her feel instantly warm inside. "I'm glad this is over for you, but I'm also a little sad that you lost the only other part of your family."

He was right. Preston Reed was the last of her biological family—at least as far as she knew.

"Frankly, I'm just glad it's over. At this point, I don't have it in me to forgive him." She worked up a smile of her own. "My plan is to get on with my life and be grateful for the good memories we were able to glean from so-called friends of my parents."

"That's an excellent way to go forward." He wrapped her arm around his. "How about we find a place to have breakfast and talk about your other plans for the future."

She leaned in close. "I was thinking we could pick up something to take back to our motel and do our talking—or not—there."

He grinned. "Much better idea."

They drove away from the police station, and Anne realized she already had a great plan in mind. She would start her own family...with this man—eventually. Maybe it was a little early in the relationship, but if life had taught her anything, it was not to put off her dreams. She smiled at Jack. As long as he was willing, of course.

He flashed her a smile and reached for her hand.

She had a feeling he was more than willing.

Chapter Twenty-One

Chicago
Monday, July 14
The Colby Agency, 10:00 a.m.

Victoria spread the *Chicago Tribune* across her desk. She smiled. Mary Morton had made the headlines. After thirty years her name had been cleared. To see this and know the agency had helped make it happen warmed her heart.

The door of her office burst open, and Jamie rushed in with her own copy of the *Tribune*. "Have you seen it?"

"I have. Great work, Jamie. I am so very proud."

Her granddaughter settled in one of the chairs in front of Victoria's desk. "I had a feeling about this one."

"Always trust your instincts," Victoria agreed.

"I understand Jack has decided to take some vacation time." Jamie's eyes twinkled.

Victoria nodded. "He has. He's been such a workaholic for years. I'm so glad he finally found the time." Or the right reason, she mused.

"I'll never tire of these happy endings," Jamie enthused.

Her granddaughter was so like her. This made Victoria inordinately happy.

Jamie folded her paper and laid it aside. "Grandmother, you and Grandpa should take a vacation too. Get out of the city and enjoy yourselves. No one works harder than the two of you. We can handle things here for a few weeks."

"A few weeks?" she repeated with raised eyebrows. How could she possibly agree to such a schedule?

Jamie inclined her head. "Two or three, I mean. It would do you both good."

Victoria's gaze narrowed. "Did your grandpa put you up to this?"

"Perhaps." Jamie grinned. "Just say yes. He has a big surprise waiting for you."

Victoria loved surprises, especially from Lucas. "Well, I suppose a little time off won't hurt."

Jamie shot to her feet. "Excellent. I'll schedule a staff meeting so you can tell the others."

Before she could say a word her granddaughter was off and running.

As much as Victoria always looked forward

to the agency's next big case, she couldn't wait to spend some well-deserved time relaxing with Lucas, the man she loved with every part of her being.

*****

Read on for an excerpt from
Witness to Murder,
*another Colby Agency: Next Generation story
coming from Debra Webb and
Harlequin Intrigue next month!*

Chapter One

Chicago
Saturday, August 9
Chicago Chop House
La Salle Drive, 11:30 p.m.

Leah Gerard had waited, seated at an elegantly set table in a barely lit well-appointed dining room, for more than thirty minutes.

Many things could be done in half an hour. She could have a leisurely lunch in that same amount of time. Or she might've read a couple of chapters in her current favorite book. For that matter, she could've vacuumed her entire apartment or had her biannual dental cleaning.

But she was doing none of those. Leah had waited thirty-three minutes now for her date to finish up his business meeting. And it was nearly midnight. This was not the way a first date should go.

She rolled her eyes. Honestly, if her best friend hadn't been on her back for weeks now about

Leah jump-starting her social life she would not have bothered with this date thing. Who had time for a social life when her final semester of graduate school started in just over a week? She needed every minute that she wasn't working to get a head start on the required reading. This was, admittedly, something she should have started weeks ago, but she'd taken every extra shift possible at work to build up her savings.

Between her share of the apartment rent and food, she barely scraped by. Once the semester began she would be forced to drop back to part-time at the library. Until then, every paid hour counted. As much as she wanted to maintain her grade point average, she also wanted to eat and have a roof over her head.

She braced her elbows on the table, rested her chin in her hands and sighed. What the heck was she even doing here?

"Good question," she muttered with mounting disgust—mostly at herself.

The dining room part of the restaurant was barely lit because the place was no longer open. The Chop House had closed at ten. Cleanup had been done and the staff had departed. Raymond, her date, had promised he would be ready to go at eleven. He'd asked Leah to meet him here so they could go straight to a nearby after-dark art exhibit that was supposedly all the rage. The gallery was only a few blocks away from the restaurant and the opening began at midnight, so they would have time for a drink before things got started.

Leah checked the time on her phone and shook her head. That would not be happening at his point. Oh well. Raymond Douglas was supposed to be a real catch. The one time she'd met him he had seemed very nice. Certainly he was handsome. And he was a rising star in the culinary world. In fact, he owned ten percent of this exclusive downtown restaurant as well as a few others. He'd met with the other investors right here tonight and stayed after closing to work out a number of issues with management. Except, apparently, things had not gone well, or surely he would be finished by now.

With a quick check of her cell phone she confirmed that he had not sent a text to explain why he was running behind or how much longer he would be. She'd done exactly as he'd said she should. She'd arrived at eleven. The last of the staff had been leaving, and no one had questioned her coming in as they hurriedly departed. She assumed Raymond had informed them that he was expecting a guest. Either that or the crew had been too tired or so happy to be off work—maybe both—that they just hadn't noticed her at all.

Leah checked the time once more: 11:40. This was inching toward ridiculous. As patient as she wanted to be, the last of hers was swiftly running out. Five more minutes, she decided. She could give him that much time. Isla Morris, her roommate and best friend, had reminded her that Raymond was no one to blow off. Leah had googled him. She had a feeling he was more playboy than she was interested in. Frankly, she was stunned he'd called her. They'd only met once. The night Isla and two of their friends had taken Leah to one of their favorite dance clubs for her birthday just two weeks ago. Isla had told Leah that she had worked at the Chop House through her undergraduate premed years which was how she'd gotten to know the guy. After the chance encounter on Leah's birthday, Raymond had called Isla and asked for Leah's contact information. And here she was.

So far the night wasn't exactly social media post worthy. Not that she posted that often. She was too busy, and frankly, she just wasn't that into online social stuff.

Next year, she told herself, life would be different. She would be finished with school, would find a great job, and life would start to shape into a good, financially secure future.

Leah occupied herself with surveying the dimly lit dining room. Most of the lights were out, but the room wasn't completely dark. There was just enough light to give anyone who walked by on the sidewalk a glimpse of high-class dining. The tables were all dressed in fresh white linens. Crystal and silver flanked elegant white plates. All was set for lunch tomorrow. Stylish, modern chandeliers hung from the towering ceiling like icicles. Sleek black marble floors were the perfect backdrop to all the white and silver. The floor-to-ceiling windows framed the vast room like a stage for passersby to admire. It was all very chic.

Enough waiting. Leah scooted back her chair and stood. With a big breath she walked across the room, weaving between the sea of tables. A thump startled her to a stop. Was that a door? Was he leaving the office finally? Should she go back to the table?

Another thump...then a series of dings like hanging stainless-steel pots swaying together.

Leah moved closer to the swinging door that led into the kitchen area. The echo of footsteps had her expecting Raymond to walk through the door before she reached it.

But he didn't.

What was he doing in there?

She stepped closer to the door, tiptoed to see through the octagon window that allowed for viewing comings and goings. Her gaze first settled on the rows of pots and pans hanging from overhead hooks. A long stainless-steel table that gleamed from its recent cleaning sat beneath them. Then...

She froze.

Blond hair...black suit jacket... Leah blinked. Raymond lay supine on the floor. The stainless-steel table blocked her view of the lower half of his body. But his upper half was right there in full view. Blue shirt...darker blue tie. Her gaze settled on his face. His eyes were open. Blood made a path down his forehead.

The air stopped flowing into her lungs.

Leah blinked again to give her brain a moment to make sense of or to refute what her eyes saw. Her lips parted, and a scream swelled in her throat.

Then he moved.

The scream deflated.

His upper body slid fully behind the table, out of her view, as if someone had grabbed him by the legs and pulled him away.

A smear of blood on the gray flooring was left in his wake.

Leah cupped her hand over her mouth to hold back the new scream that burgeoned.

Footsteps and another thump echoed.

Abject fear sent adrenaline rushing through her veins.

Run.

Leah turned around to run and stalled once more.

Don't make a sound.

She forced herself to move more slowly and silently as she wove through the tables and toward the entrance. Her heart pounded harder with each step. Her body weak with relief, she pushed against the doors. They didn't move.

The heavy wooden set of French doors were locked.

Ice formed inside her. *What now? What now?*

She eased away from the door and the hostess station. Head spinning, she hunkered down behind a table. There had to be an emergency exit somewhere...

Think!

In the corridor where the bathrooms were located, maybe.

Or was it?

She'd never been here before, but she had gone to the ladies' room when she first arrived to check her hair and makeup. She closed her eyes and called to mind that short corridor. There had been an emergency exit there...right? *Yes.*

But that corridor was on the other side of the dining room. Staring across that expanse now it seemed miles away.

Another indistinct sound came from the kitchen.

Didn't matter how far to the exit...she had to get out of here.

Heart thumping wildly, she got down onto all fours. Tugged up the skirt of the black cocktail dress she'd chosen for this date and then crawled along the floor. She couldn't risk standing up again. If whoever was back there glanced through that kitchen door window he would see her. She remained on all fours, rushing around and between the tables as quickly as the building terror would allow. When she reached the corridor, she almost cried out with relief.

Once she was in that short hall, she dared to stand.

Even before she reached the emergency exit she saw the sign—opening the door triggered an alarm. The killer would hear the alarm. He would know someone was here...a potential witness.

Defeat sucked the wind out of her.

Desperate, she eased into the ladies' room. She wished there was a lock on the main door, but there was not. She hurried into one of the stalls and locked that door for the good it would do if someone wanted to get in. It was meager protection, but it was the best she could do. Leah drew in a steadying breath and used her cell phone to call 911.

As soon as the dispatcher recited her spiel,

Leah whispered, "My name is Leah Gerard. I'm at the Chop House on La Salle Drive. Someone murdered Raymond Douglas. Whoever killed him is still in the restaurant. Please...help me." A keening sound rose from the depths of her soul.

"Are you safe?" the dispatcher asked calmly.

Leah forced her mind to focus. "I... I don't know. I'm in the ladies' room locked in a stall. I don't think he knows I'm here." She listened intently for sound beyond the ladies' room. Nothing. "Please hurry."

"Did you see or hear a weapon?"

"No," Leah murmured.

"Are you armed, Ms. Gerard?"

"No. Please. Hurry."

The dispatcher assured Leah a unit was already en route to her location. She was to stay in place and on the line until help arrived.

Then Leah did the only thing she could...she waited.

Copyright © 2025 by Debra Webb

Get up to 4 Free Books!

We'll send you 2 free books from each series you try PLUS a free Mystery Gift.

Both the **Harlequin Intrigue®** and **Harlequin® Romantic Suspense** series feature compelling novels filled with heart-racing action-packed romance that will keep you on the edge of your seat.

YES! Please send me 2 FREE novels from the Harlequin Intrigue or Harlequin Romantic Suspense series and my FREE gift (gift is worth about $10 retail). After receiving them, if I don't wish to receive any more books, I can return the shipping statement marked "cancel." If I don't cancel, I will receive 6 brand-new Harlequin Intrigue Larger-Print books every month and be billed just $7.19 each in the U.S. or $7.99 each in Canada, or 4 brand-new Harlequin Romantic Suspense books every month and be billed just $6.39 each in the U.S. or $7.19 each in Canada, a savings of 20% off the cover price. It's quite a bargain! Shipping and handling is just 50¢ per book in the U.S. and $1.25 per book in Canada.* I understand that accepting the 2 free books and gift places me under no obligation to buy anything. I can always return a shipment and cancel at any time by calling the number below. The free books and gift are mine to keep no matter what I decide.

Choose one:
- ☐ **Harlequin Intrigue Larger-Print** (199/399 BPA G36Y)
- ☐ **Harlequin Romantic Suspense** (240/340 BPA G36Y)
- ☐ **Or Try Both!** (199/399 & 240/340 BPA G36Z)

Name (please print)

Address   Apt. #

City   State/Province   Zip/Postal Code

Email: Please check this box ☐ if you would like to receive newsletters and promotional emails from Harlequin Enterprises ULC and its affiliates. You can unsubscribe anytime.

Mail to the Harlequin Reader Service:
IN U.S.A.: P.O. Box 1341, Buffalo, NY 14240-8531
IN CANADA: P.O. Box 603, Fort Erie, Ontario L2A 5X3

Want to explore our other series or interested in ebooks? Visit www.ReaderService.com or call 1-800-873-8635.

*Terms and prices subject to change without notice. Prices do not include sales taxes, which will be charged (if applicable) based on your state or country of residence. Canadian residents will be charged applicable taxes. Offer not valid in Quebec. This offer is limited to one order per household. Books received may not be as shown. Not valid for current subscribers to the Harlequin Intrigue or Harlequin Romantic Suspense series. All orders subject to approval. Credit or debit balances in a customer's account(s) may be offset by any other outstanding balance owed by or to the customer. Please allow 4 to 6 weeks for delivery. Offer available while quantities last.

Your Privacy—Your information is being collected by Harlequin Enterprises ULC, operating as Harlequin Reader Service. For a complete summary of the information we collect, how we use this information and to whom it is disclosed, please visit our privacy notice located at https://corporate.harlequin.com/privacy-notice. Notice to California Residents – Under California law, you have specific rights to control and access your data. For more information on these rights and how to exercise them, visit https://corporate.harlequin.com/california-privacy. For additional information for residents of other U.S. states that provide their residents with certain rights with respect to personal data, visit https://corporate.harlequin.com/other-state-residents-privacy-rights/.